Baked Alaska
and other
Short Short Stories

with Whimsy, Humor, and Tongue-in-Cheek for your Guestroom Bedside Table

Daniel Hoyt Daniels

iUniverse, Inc.
New York   Bloomington

Baked Alaska and other Short Short Stories with Whimsy, Humor, and Tongue-in-Cheek for your Guestroom Bedside Table

This is a work of fiction. All of the characters, names, incidents, organizations, and dialogue in these stories are either the products of the author's imagination or are used fictitiously.

iUniverse books may be ordered through booksellers or by contacting:

iUniverse
1663 Liberty Drive
Bloomington, IN 47403
www.iuniverse.com
1-800-Authors (1-800-288-4677)

Because of the dynamic nature of the Internet, any Web addresses or links contained in this book may have changed since publication and may no longer be valid. The views expressed in this work are solely those of the author and do not necessarily reflect the views of the publisher, and the publisher hereby disclaims any responsibility for them.

ISBN: 978-1-4502-0172-8 (sc)
ISBN: 978-1-4502-0173-5 (ebk)

Printed in the United States of America

iUniverse rev. date: 4/5/2010

Contents

Baked Alaska 1

Heads I Win, Tails I Win 9

Stormy Night - A Story of Fear.........................13

Good News 17

The Live Oak 21

The Rabbit 25

Bitches on the Beach 29

Hello There! 33

Playing It Cool 39

Making Arrangements 43

That's Okay 49

Anything You Want..53

Getting Even 59

Hasta La Vista 63

It Wouldn't Be Advisable 69

A New Start 77

The Prodigal Calf 85

A Few More Days..91

Like I Said, an Ordinary Guy 101

Turkey in the Straw 107

John Harvard Fantoma....................................113

My Brother-In-Law Is a Jerk...........................121

The Moustache...125

Money Money Money.....................................131

The World of Art..139

The Beard..145

Bastille Day – Proving a Point 153

Locks of Gold..163

Hypocrisy, Anyone ?......................................175

You Took the Words.......................................183

Preface

These little stories are all fictional works originally written for the amusement and pleasure of the author and his friends. Most of them are completely imaginary, although some of them may have originated from a seed of truth. They can be read aloud in ten or fifteen minutes, which is the approximate amount of time allotted to each participant attending the periodic meetings of the Beaufort (South Carolina) Writers' Group, under the helpful guidance and encouragement of Ethard Van Stee, the organizer and stylish director of the group. The stories are all unrelated to one another. If the same name appears in more than one story, it is not to be implied that it is the same character.

I would like to thank Martha Lawrence and the editors at iUniverse for their helpful suggestions. Any errors are of course my own. Comments on these pieces, or requests for reproduction or other use of them, will be welcomed by the author.

Daniel Hoyt Daniels
P. O. Box 1681
Beaufort, SC 29901
December, 2009

Baked Alaska

When I crawled through the narrow opening into that Alaskan igloo, I never dreamed what was in store for me and how it would change my life.

Alaska . . . ! The word alone has always filled me with a sense of adventure, standing as it does for all that is exotic, vast, wild, unknown, exciting. It conjures up images of Jack London and his dog Buck, half dog and half wolf; and Robert Service and Sam Magee from Tennessee. And fishing through the ice, and polar bears and seals. And gold, and sled races, and great herds of caribou migrating across the vast snow-covered plains in the shadow of Mt. McKinley, or Denali, as the natives call it. The natives. They call themselves Inuits - most of them do. I call them Eskimos.

And fresh cool air, with that invigorating nip that brings you alive. And stars. Alaska has stars like you have never seen before. I have read that in any one clear night you can see between six and eight TIMES as many stars in Alaska as you can see in Oregon. I think I was in love with Alaska before I ever went there.

Oregon. O - Ree - Gun! Would you believe, although I was born and brought up in Oregon, until last year I had never been to Alaska? Never . . . been . . . to . . . Alaska!

Well, one day last fall my cousin Barbara came over to the house with a newspaper thing tucked under her arm and said, "Dan, I'm thinking of going to Alaska. Elderhostel has this deal where you go to Juneau and

Anchorage and then Fairbanks. Eight days. Four of them in Fairbanks. You HAVE to come, because you're fifty-five and I'm not."

It didn't take much persuasion, as images from my youthful dreams of adventure in the wilds flashed across my inward eye. The next day we booked in with Elderhostel for their November trip. "Alaska Adventure," it was called. With discount rates for off season.

We went to Juneau first, which reminded me of my visit to the New England coast a few years ago. It's a charming little seaside town - cute, historic, art-y - almost touristy. It could have been Gloucester, or Newburyport, or Bar Harbor, only the hills were bigger, mountains really, and came right down to the water's edge. And it wasn't even very cold. Just around thirty-two degrees.

Anchorage was a lot colder, closer to zero, but nevertheless it reminded me of Amarillo Texas - Amarillo on the sea - an orderly and familiar looking development of square city streets and office buildings that did not fit at all with my image of what Alaska should be like.

So I was really looking forward to Fairbanks. Fairbanks is in the vast northern valley, near the Yukon River. It's the "outback" of Alaska. But even Fairbanks had its hotels and chain-stores. Even had McDonalds. Can you imagine! Way up there in the sticks. McDonalds! In the middle of Alaska. I could have stayed in Oregon for that.

We had Elderhostel tour guides or lecturers at all these places, telling us about the history of the land, about the early Russian settlements, about the gold rush, about the importance of the fisheries and lumbering industries and of course the oil, and about how different the culture of the real Eskimos was from that of the white man.

So when they offered an optional two-day side trip to the outlying Eskimo village of Chatanika, I was the first to sign up. Chatanika, they said, had real Eskimo igloos. Made of ice. Real ice houses. With its higher elevation on the mountain slopes above the valley, Chatanika was colder, much colder, even than Fairbanks.

But what a view! In the distance you could see the path of the mighty Yukon River, frozen and covered with snow, gently spreading out in sinusoidal loops as it meandered over the valley floor, twenty or thirty miles away to the southwest, shining white and pink in the late afternoon sun. "Late afternoon" came early in those latitudes - it was only a quarter after two, but the sun was already scraping the horizon.

There couldn't have been more than seventy or eighty dwellings in all of what was called Chatanika. A number of them were igloos, but they were widely separated and were spread out over an area of several miles across the upper valley. It was hard even to see them against the white background of the snow.

Barbara and I were assigned quarters in an igloo belonging to a young widow lady, named Aleta, who lived a simple life in a remote area, much as her parents and grandparents had lived. Her husband had been killed two or three years before, during a polar bear hunting expedition, but Aleta had sworn that she would never give up her igloo home. She could not, she said, bear the thought of another person possessing it. She would rather see it destroyed.

I can't say much more for the little house of ice than that it was cozy . . . with bear skins made into rugs and blankets, and caribou skins made into curtains that separated different parts of the house for privacy. It was really just one big room. Seats were made out of leather cushions. And a large round leather ottoman-sort-of centerpiece served as a table. Spartan but functional. And, relatively speaking, it was warmer inside. At least we were out of the wind. But still, to me, it was cold in there. If you touched the icy walls, they were - as my mother would have said - as cold as ice.

But I haven't told you about Aleta. Our hostess, Aleta. When she threw back the furry parka from around her cheeks, I saw the most beautiful face I could ever have imagined. And out here, miles from nowhere! I couldn't believe it. It may sound corny, but her skin was as white as snow and her eyes shone like diamonds in the sky. Barbara had to give me an elbow in the ribs, whispering for me to stop staring.

And then, when she took the parka off, I . . . well, I looked some more - a good bit more - in spite of Barbara's surreptitious jabs. She was short, though taller than most Eskimos, and rather well-rounded. And if her figure, as I visualized it under her leather blouse and breeches, was not perfection, it must have been pretty close. Yes, dear Reader, I was suddenly in love. Suddenly and completely. Smitten. In love. Even with Barbara there looking at me.

For the rest of our visit I forced myself to behave myself, while Aleta told us of the rugged life that she and her people had had to lead in past years. But what she was attached to was her little home, which she rarely left except for an occasional two-day or three-day visit to

Fairbanks for supplies and news and a little chit-chat. She could not bear to face the rigors of life in the outback of Alaska if she did not have her cozy home. This home.

"Where would you go if you didn't live here?" I asked her.

"I really have no place to go. I would probably let the Gods blow me anywhere they wanted to - Timbuktu, Australia, Oregon - anywhere."

I had to wonder whether she knew where any of those places were. "Oregon?" I said, "Why Oregon?"

"I don't know," she said. "It just popped into my head. I guess it's one of those out-of-the-way places you hear of sometimes. But that word, Oregon, O - Ree - Gun - it does have an exotic sound, doesn't it . . . ?"

Strange, I thought. Was this an omen from the Gods? I had never told her I was from Oregon; never said anything about it. How can Oregon be so famous all around the world? That was a question I never did answer. "Does the cold bother you?" I asked. "It's pretty cold here, even inside." I still had my heavy coat on, and I kept it on the whole time we were there.

"Not really . . . yes, I guess it does at that. In fact, I dream of being warm. But for me, it's only a dream, for this is my home. It's all I have, in this life anyway . . . Perhaps in another life . . . " Her voice trailed off. She smiled, sort of a dreamy smile, and, in spite of my reputation for brazen effrontery, I had to lower my eyes and turn my head.

"We had better be leaving," said Barbara, with her perspicacious insight and penetrating woman's intuition. And leave we did.

But, believe it or not, Aleta rubbed noses with us before we left. Rubbed noses! I thought they only did that in fairy stories or movies about Eskimos. But she did it, first to Barbara, and then to me. A little longer for me, I noticed. Or was it just my imagination?

Oh, the pain of leaving that woman! Even though I had never even held her in my arms, or given her a proper kiss, I began to imagine that she was someone I would like to have as my wife - someone I would be happy to spend the rest of my life with. But here . . . ? In Chatanika . . . ? In an IGLOO . . . ? The thought was madness.

Arriving home two days later, and basking in the soothing warmth of Oregon's forty-degree weather, I tried to think. This woman was constantly on my mind. Poor Aleta, there in her beloved igloo. I should give her something nice - something that she would remember. So after seventy-two hours of concentrated effort and very little sleep, I finally got my brain in gear and decided what my gift should be.

Over the next few days I went shopping and bought several fairly large items, and had them packed for shipment to Alaska. Then I took them to Federal Express, who claim they can deliver to any place in the world. I tried to explain exactly where Chatanika was, and showed them on the map in order to be sure. There. Just fifty miles north of Fairbanks. Frankly, I was somewhat surprised when they accepted my order.

Then I wrote to her, saying I was worried about her, and telling her I was sending her a heater for her igloo. It was a 220-volt General Electric heater, 1200 BTU's, very reliable. But as it needed a power source in that isolated area, I was sending a portable gasoline-driven generator along with it. I had found a cute little Briggs and Stratton four-stroke, ten-hp model that at full blast could barely have turned out 5000 watts, although that probably would have been enough to light up half the town of Chatanika. And I also sent a five-gallon drum of gasoline to be sure that she had something to get started with until she could find replenishment.

Actually I hoped replenishment would not be necessary.

Federal Express wasn't too happy with the gasoline, but with a fat tip to the clerk and my assurance that there was no possibility of a leak in my expensive German-made canister, I got the whole shebang underway.

Then I had to wait. I waited almost a month, until, one day, I got a telegram from Aleta. I didn't even know there were still such things as telegrams anymore. Anyway, the telegram read as follows:

RECEIVED YOUR ENORMOUS CRATES STOP NOW READING INSTRUCTIONS STOP YOU ARE MOST KIND STOP I LIKE YOU VERY MUCH STOP LETTER FOLLOWS

Yes, I had sent instructions along with the crates. Oh . . . one thing I didn't tell you about was the timer device that I included. The timer was designed to go on and off during the day or night, so as not to overheat the igloo. After all, it might be disastrous if an igloo made of ice got too hot. And then, if Aleta should leave the igloo for twenty-four hours or more, she could set the timer to turn the heat completely off, so as not to damage the ice walls.

Again, I waited. Of course, the mail from Chatanika, even a letter, could take two weeks or more. But I never learned whether there was a letter on the way, for, only ten days after the first telegram, I received another. It was pretty long, certainly the longest telegram I have ever gotten.

DEAR DANIEL STOP DISASTER HAS STRUCK STOP I FOLLOWED YOUR INSTRUCTIONS STOP HAD TO LEAVE THREE DAYS FOR FAIRBANKS STOP ON RETURN FOUND HEATER STILL GOING FULL-BLAST IN MIDDLE OF BIG PUDDLE OF WATER STOP NO MORE IGLOO STOP TIMER DEVICE APPARENTLY FAULTY STOP ARRIVING PORTLAND OREGON VIA ALASKAN AIRLINES FLT 843 DEC 24, 16:30 HOURS PACIFIC TIME STOP NO OTHER PLACE TO GO STOP

A feeling of warmth flowed over me such as I had never known since the day I crawled into that igloo six weeks earlier. Of course I was there to meet Alaskan Airlines flight 843. And she was as beautiful as ever. And we spent Christmas in a warm ski lodge at the foot of Mt. Hood. And we were married New Year's Eve. And we are very happy, looking forward to a long life together.

And, oh, one other thing. After we had been married a couple of months, she said to me one evening, "You know, Dan, isn't it lucky that the timer switch had that malfunction? Otherwise, I wouldn't even be here, and we wouldn't be married, or anything."

I put on my straight face and my best Mona-Lisa smile. "What malfunction?" I said. "There wasn't any malfunction."

THE END

Heads I Win, Tails I Win

It was never a big deal, but when I was a kid there was a game we used to play that I could almost always win. It was called matching pennies, a game for two. There were different ways you could play it. One way was for each kid to stack ten pennies in his fingers, and one kid would choose "same" and the other would choose "different." They would go through the stacks together, one penny at a time, and if they matched, the "same" kid won; otherwise the "different" kid won. Another way, one that I liked more because I was better at it, was to have a "tosser" flip a coin and the "caller" say heads or tails. Usually we played "for funsies," but sometimes we played "for keeps." I liked being caller because I could usually win six or seven out of ten, sometimes eight. I even called ten in a row once. That won me ten cents and lost me a friend.

Then we moved and I went to a different school and forgot about the matching pennies game for many years. In college I took some business courses and when I graduated I got a job with an investment brokerage firm as a "researcher." "Gopher" would have been a better description. Anyway, it supported me and after two or three years I even got promoted to "associate investment analyst" with a boost in salary and a chance to do a little investing on my own account. By now I was married and living in a rented apartment in town. Later on, about the time the twins were born, some of the investments in my personal account really shot up. I suddenly had enough money for a down-payment on an expensive home in the suburbs, and at the rate I was going I would have my mortgage paid off in no time.

Then came the crash of 1987. I don't know where you were in 1987, but believe me, working in a brokerage house with clients screaming at you and your own money invested in a highly leveraged margin account is not where you would want to be. My firm's official view was that the drop in the stock market was just a "minor fluctuation" or a "market-driven adjustment" caused by "profit-taking" and "technical factors." So I hung on, and when the margin calls started coming in I met them as long as I could. I would have felt pretty stupid if I had sold out and the market bounced back two weeks later and started setting new highs again. But it didn't bounce back. And soon I was faced with margin calls amounting to almost $40,000 which I didn't have.

Now, I have always been an honest man, and I have always worked hard, and through my research I KNEW my investments were sound and that my share values would soon pick up. I certainly wasn't going to go out and steal $40,000 somewhere, but neither could I afford to sell out now and take that loss, not with a wife and twin boys and - did I mention - another on the way. And a big house with a big mortgage. I just had to borrow $40,000 somewhere until I could pay it back.

I debated whether I should tell Marie, my wife, of my problems, but she already suspected the truth. Besides, I have never kept any secrets from her, so I told her.

That evening something happened. By chance we heard on the local news that a neighbor had won $150,000 at Las Vegas the previous weekend. The report quoted him as saying he had won it slowly. "Just a penny at a time," were his words. A silly figure of speech, obviously, but . . . But it rang a bell.

I told Marie to get out some pennies to see if I still had the old sixth sense of winning the matching game, or rather her tossing and me calling. Immediately I got fifty-seven right out of the first hundred. Then sixty-one. Then sixty-two. Then fifty-seven again. We kept on, and out of one thousand calls I got five hundred and ninety-eight right, almost a 60-40 win ratio. I still had the old knack.

I began to calculate how much of a stake I would need and how long it would take to win $40,000 at roulette. If I could win at heads and tails, I could win at red and black, or odd and even.

I figured that playing slowly and carefully I could double my money in two or three days at the roulette wheel. Roulette takes time, and I could not afford to rush it. There was a long three-day weekend coming up, and I could fly to Vegas late Friday afternoon and come back Monday evening. But where could I borrow the $40,000 I needed for my stake?

Then the answer hit me. It was obvious. All I had to do was make a Friday "accounting error" in one of my million-dollar client accounts and make a "correcting adjustment" Tuesday morning. No one hurt, no money lost or unaccounted for, everything hunky-dory. So I did it.

At 3:00 p.m. Friday old John P. Witherspoon's account showed $3,492,333. At 3:05 p.m. Friday it showed $3,450,333, a drop of $42,000. By 10:30 a.m. Tuesday it would again show $3,492,333.

I am not a greedy person, and I had no desire to try to make a killing like "the man who broke the bank at Monte Carlo." I have heard that those places have people who watch big winners closely - you break the bank one day and they break your knees the next. None of that for me. I just needed $40,000 to carry me through this one hard time. So I packed my bag, kissed Marie goodbye, and went to the airport with $42,000 in my pocket, including $2,000 for airfare and expenses.

I would play three roulette tables at once, for they are notoriously slow in turn-around time. That way, if I kept my 60-40 win ratio, I would double my stake in just two days, maybe less. If I slipped to 59-41, or even 58-42, I had the third day to make up for it.

As it turned out, I stayed all three days, then flew home.

Marie met me at the airport. "How did it go?" she asked.

"40-60," I replied.

"Great," she said, "then you did it! That's just what you were aiming for!"

"You don't understand. I said 40-60, not 60-40."

THE END

Stormy Night ~ A Story of Fear

Maybe I could have been a comedian. But I don't think I was cut out to be a Shakespearean actor. I was only nine at the time of this story, although I was big for my age and already in the fifth grade.

I'm older now, much older, but not as smart. I think that that must have been my peak, and that my smarts have been going downhill ever since. But at that time I was the top kid in my math class. So, with infallible pedagogical logic, they picked me for a big part in the school play coming up that spring.

The title of the play was "The Little Hams Do Hamlet." (Good Grief!) The parts and the scenes were all cut up and passed around so no kid had to say too much. I got given a bunch of weird lines beginning with "To be or not to be . . ." which I was told to memorize. It was called a soliloquy and was about this guy Hamlet, who was mad. I mean, really mad - mad enough at his mother-f . . . ing stepfather to want to kill him, but couldn't make up his mind to do it.

But I am not good at memorizing stuff, and I told my teacher I didn't think I could go through with it. It wasn't like math, which was something you did because it was logical and where you didn't have to just memorize things. She insisted I COULD do it, and said I HAD to, for our reputation and honor - words like that - reputation and honor, of Jones Elementary School, J-E-S, "jeese." (We kids called going to school "going to Jesus," but of course we never let our parents or teachers know that.)

Anyway, I worked on it for a couple of days, and it wasn't so hard to learn as I had feared. I got so I could say it straight through in the shower in the morning. But even so, I was afraid. How do you know that something you can do in the morning in the shower at home is something you can do in the evening at the school auditorium with all the other kids looking at you, and all their parents looking at you, and all the teachers looking at you, and Mrs. Abernathy from the school cafeteria there looking at you, and even the principal - Mister Grunt was his name - there looking at you?

And fear seized me, and I was sure I would forget my lines, and I even threw up at the breakfast table just thinking about it, although I had gone through the whole thing without a mistake in the shower a few minutes before. That was on a Monday, and the show was to be the next Friday night at seven o'clock. Eat an early supper, we were told. But what if I threw up my early supper right there on the stage? Right in front of all those people? And what are you supposed to do if you forget your lines? Vanish into thin air?

Tuesday afternoon I stayed after school to tell my teacher I couldn't do it. By now I was a walking wreck; I had the fear jitters and the fear shakes so bad I had to go to the bathroom about once an hour, and every day it was getting worse. Just waiting to tell her made my palms sweat and brought stomach acid to the back of my throat.

"You'll be fine," she said, "you're smart."

"No I'm not!" I said. "I'm dumb, I'm dumb, I'm dumb!" What I meant was "I'm scared, I'm scared, I'm scared."

She said, let me hear you try some of it now, so I did. I started right off, "To be or not to be, that is the question" - and it wasn't really hard at all, with her there, with her encouraging smile. I just went right through it, like in the shower. Maybe I could do it after all!

But that evening, at home, I kept hearing the words as I was trying to eat supper. It was as though the words were coming up and meeting the food in my mouth trying to go down, and neither of them getting through. And it continued more or less like that right up until Friday. I could hardly eat or sleep or do anything but worry about whether I might forget my lines up there on that stage. I was really scared. I could say them all right when I didn't HAVE to - as long as I wasn't eating at the same time. But how did I know I could do it when I DID have to? Up there in front of all those people? The truth is I was terrified. And you don't have to tell anybody this, but I even wet myself. Thursday night, thinking about it, the night before the show was to go on.

Friday was the nightmare of nightmares. I staggered blindly through the day like a zombie, saying, "to be or not to be" and all that to myself over and over again, but still possessed by the fear that I wouldn't be able to do it that evening, and that people would laugh. Not laugh WITH me, but laugh AT me.

As you can imagine, I couldn't eat any supper, not right before we were to go on stage. As the time for my entrance approached, my palms went into a sweat again, my temples throbbed, and my knees shook, even though my teacher was there behind me, watching, saying softly, encouragingly, "You can do it; you can do it." She always makes me feel good and, you know, I began to believe her.

When my time came and I was alone on the stage, with one hundred and eighty pairs of attentive ears cupped in my direction, I felt my throat relax and my knees strengthen. I lifted up my chin and took on a pensive, Shakespearean look as I had been told to do. I had overcome my fear.

I opened my mouth to let the words pour freely forth, and out they came:

"It was a dark and normy stite . . . "

THE END

Epilogue

I stopped, lost, not knowing what I had said or where I was. There was pin-drop silence. Then, after about ten seconds, the hall went into thunderous laughter and applause. It was - as they said when the Titanic went down - it was a night to remember.

And that is why I say that, if I had chosen to follow the theatre as a career, it would have been as a comedian. The ability to make people laugh is an uncommon gift.

Good News

Finally the phone rang.

I had been waiting for her call and dashed across the room to pick it up with a light heart and joyful anticipation. I was happy - happier than I had ever been before in my life. Let me tell you how I found such happiness.

I was terribly shy as a lad, knew nothing about women, or girls as they were known as then, and I was married very young to the first woman who gave me a tumble. Jane Morrison. It was the gentlemanly thing to do under the circumstances, but it was a mistake. A big mistake.

There were dozens of differences in our values, our outlooks, our interests, the greatest of which was money. Jane never had enough, was obsessed with the idea of having more. She even got us to take out million-dollar accidental life insurance policies. When our premature baby, James, reached 21 and graduated from college, Jane and I acknowledged the truth between us, that there was no longer anything holding us together, and got a legal separation. Divorce was out of the question because of our religion. Our hypocritical religion. But there it was.

Her lawyer was smarter than mine, and when the smoke cleared, I found that the separation agreement I had signed gave her a big chunk of my monthly salary, but I was glad for the new-found freedom in my life, a relief after years of living a charade, pretending to friends and relatives that we were really the happy couple whose face we fabricated for the outside world.

And, yes, I met someone else. Marie was everything Jane was not; Marie did not put on airs, she was interested in community affairs, she was athletic, read widely, and we COMMUNICATED. And this time I really was in love. But I couldn't marry her. Jane still clung to her religion thing and would not contemplate divorce. And although by then she was seeing other men, I think she enjoyed knowing she held me a helpless hostage. This situation went on for months that gradually turned into years.

As my love for Marie grew, so did my frustration, for although I was quite willing to accept a divorce, I was too old-fashioned to actually live with a woman not my wife. An angry pressure slowly built up in my mind against Jane, and I even dreamed of how perfect life would be if I could somehow get rid of her. But I am not a violent man, quite the contrary, and I shuddered at the thought of my own thoughts. I could never do anything like that.

Moving quickly on with my story: last week Jane and three of her friends were on a cruise ship to Antarctica that hit an iceberg and went straight to the bottom, just like the *Titanic*. All hands lost, 437 passengers and crew. At first I was shocked, deeply sorry, and even remorseful, almost guilt-ridden for the feelings I had harbored toward Jane. But gradually my heart lightened, as I repeated to myself that, after all, it wasn't my fault. I felt a freedom and positive brightness that I had never known before as I realized that a millstone had been removed from my neck. Now I could plan my own life and my own future!

I thought of Marie - of me and Marie - and I saw a golden sunrise; I was the happiest man you could imagine. Nothing now to prevent our being married. That is what I had been dreaming of - only dreaming of

- for months. Added to that, a surprise gift fell upon us from the insurance company, for Jane had never changed my name as beneficiary on her million-dollar accidental death policy.

I had to share my joy with Marie - I rushed to the phone; I would ask her to marry me. Now! As soon as possible.

No answer. I left a brief message on her answering machine, didn't say why I was calling, just said for her to call me, that I had something important to talk to her about. I poured a glass of wine and tried to stay calm. Marie should be calling back soon. So I waited by the phone, thinking of the words I would use to pop the question: "Will you marry me?" or "We can get married now," or "Are you doing anything tonight?" I waited about an hour for her call, although it seemed twice as long.

And then the phone rang.

"Hello, Marie?" I said.

"No," a man's voice answered. "Is that Mr. Osborne?"

"Yes. Who is this?"

"My name is Kevin McGrath. I have good news for you."

I hadn't expected approval of the insurance claim to arrive this soon, but why should I look a gift horse in the mouth?

"Yes? Go ahead . . . "

"I'm calling from the Southern Cross Steamship Company. Your wife has been found."

THE END

Epilogue

It turned out that not all hands were lost, but that there were three survivors who were picked up by a tiny Chilean fishing vessel with no radio and taken to the nearest port, Stanley Town, in the Falkland Islands. Three survivors out of four hundred and thirty-seven. Of course Jane would be one of them. She is a survivor.

The Live Oak

Some people believe oak trees can't talk. They're right. We can't. Some people believe oak trees can't think. They're wrong. We CAN think. We can think but we can't talk. Some people can talk but can't think. I know. I'm an oak tree. I think I'm an oak tree and therefore I am. But not just any oak tree. I am a live oak, a special breed. We never shed all our leaves and we never forget an insult. But we also have special powers. For instance, where do you think mistletoe gets its magical properties from? And we have other powers as well.

I was born about the time the Spaniards expelled the Moors from Spain, which was in 1492. (You can also use that date to remember when Columbus discovered America, for it was the same year.) I came from an acorn that dropped from my daddy's tree. He was already over four hundred years old, and he came from an acorn HIS daddy dropped about the time William the Conqueror was invading England in 1066. Anyway, my daddy and many of his brothers and cousins and nephews went into construction of the finest sailing vessels that ever floated on the seven seas. And I had brothers who gave their limbs for vessels that fought in the Civil War. On both sides.

Now, I never took sides in that war, not for a long time. I thought that it was an unnecessary war and that it was unnecessary to cut down and cut up so many of my brothers to make warships. But then something happened. I participated in that war, although reluctantly. They made me do it. It was near the end of the war and I am ashamed of my involvement, involuntary though it was.

Late in the year 1864 a young captain of the 3rd Battalion, 23rd Regiment of Alabama Militia was home on a week's leave, seeing his wife and young children for the first time in over two years. He was Captain Barnwell Toombs. Maybe you have heard of him. Anyway, while he was home, at dawn one day a squad of Yankees came riding through his gate with plunder in their eyes and lust in their hearts. Barnwell's instinct was to grab his rifle to fend them off as best he could, but of course he was soon overwhelmed.

Now the saddest part of this tale is that Barnwell was sentenced to death as a spy because he was out of uniform (in his pyjamas at 5:30 a.m.) with a weapon in his hand, the two factors which together meet the definition of a "spy." Out of uniform and with a weapon. He was tried by a Kangaroo Court and summarily executed by hanging on the 11th of November, 1864. My part in this was that I had to let them use one of my branches as the gallows. How could such a despicable deed ever be atoned for?

Then it came home to me that perhaps this question was not completely rhetorical after all. In the 1980's and 1990's the Yankees undertook a restoration project on their most famous sailing warship, the USS *Constitution*, in Boston Harbor. The *Constitution* had been built with timber from my ancestors and my ancestors' relatives. Solid oak, she was, with sides that were said to be almost as strong as iron and gave her the nickname "Old Ironsides." She was still afloat, but needing replacement of some weakened timber in vital areas.

The Yankees came to me and a few of my cousins for new oak timbers to do the reconstruction work. And they were the descendants of the Yankees who had abused my neutrality in 1864 and forced me into participation in that ineffably despicable deed still burning in my memory. Now was my opportunity to seek retribution.

When the men came to take me for timber, they began to mark beams for specific locations on the *Constitution*. I had within me many strong beams, but also some weak ones where I had let red-headed woodpeckers and caterpillars hollow out their nests within my wooden mansion, and I knew which beams would be strong and which would be hollow and weak. I knew the weaker beams would not last long.

When the timbers got to Boston, I made sure that the weaker beams went to the critical areas at the waterline and at the turn of the bilge, for I knew that they would give way in about twenty years. The ugly memory of my participation in the shameful incident of Capt. Toombs's hanging would be washed with the tea-stained waters of Boston Harbor and I could die in peace. Even live oaks don't live forever, but we like to know accounts will be appropriately settled after we are gone.

THE END

Epilogue

News Item, *The Boston Globe*, Tuesday, November 12, 2014: All of Boston and much of the nation are grieved this morning to learn that the most famous ship ever to serve in the United States Navy capsized and sank in Boston Harbor yesterday afternoon. The USS *Constitution*, which had been in commission in the Navy for two hundred and seventeen years, went down at sunset shortly before 5 p.m., under conditions not yet fully understood. Naval experts are investigating the cause of the catastrophe, but preliminary indications suggest the probability of faulty materials among the oak timbers used in the repair and restoration undertaken in the 1980's and 1990's. (See photos, p B-1).

The Rabbit

(Note: *The narrator is a fifteen-year-old country girl who lives in Beaufort County, South Carolina, near the Jasper County line. She tells of an event that, although she did not know it, would bring a dramatic change in her life.)*

Ever sinc I got in Middle School it seem lak it alway stars off the same way wen we goes back to school in Setember. Least ways, thas the way it seem in are school. Ise in the eigth grade now but this be the foth time I statted back to Midle School in Setember cause I hed to do the seven grade twict, mosly cause of math and aritmitic and frashuns. I can count real good and I knos how to make change an all, but when we got to frashuns I din kno whut they was talking abuot. I doan kno whut good they be's anyways. A peice of pie is ethur biger or smaller or the same as anothur peice of pie as far as I can cee.

Anyways the furs thing they mak us do in Setember was allways to rite sum thing they called a compsition for English class. When we statted the seven grade we rote abuot "Whut we did las summer." I statted the seven grade twict, so I rote abuot what I did las summer twict. It was the same compsition becase we did the same thing ever summer which was nuthing but helping to weed the tomatoe patch and the meluns or suing on the suing we made with a tire hangen frum the oak tree when are chors were dun or our Momma wuz out an not waching us.

Sum of the ritch kids thet caim to are school in buses frum the othur side of town rote abuot going to the beech

25

for the sumer. I saw the ocean onct, when we gone to my gran mothers house to see her when she dyed wen I wuz seven. It wuz realy big. I meen ther wuz more water their then you could shak a stik at. But that wunt las sumer so I cunt rite abuot that.

Anyways las year my teacher got mad at me an acused me of copping frum my compistion the yere before wich wuz true becuze we jes do the same thing ever sumer anyways.

Statt in in the eigth grade we had to rite abuot sum thing that changt yur life alot. Well, nuthing ever changt my life all tho I wisht it wood. I gues the too most important things in my life is my frens at scholl and my Momma. I din have a father. I gues I did but not one I new of.

I licked boys better then girls cause thay wuz more innerestid in you. The boys I licked best wuz in Hi Scholl wich wuz jes a nother part of are school bilding wher the middle scholl wuz. I licked the hi scholl boys beter then the chilesht kids in my own clas cause thay was older and new more an sum times had sum mony an one had a car and thay licked to driv a round an do stuff.

An a nother thing. Ther had ben sum deseases going round the county that sumer, you kno, people geting sik frum sum thing an ketching it frum each other. So after we statted scholl in Setember an I wuz finilly in the eigth grade we all hade to go to the scholl dispensry to hav tes dun. I din kno zackly whut it wuz thay wuz tessing for, but it din' hurt. A cup la weeks later thay tole us whut the resuls wuz, an that din mean much to me nethur. But thay also put it on a sheat of payper an I wuz suposed to tak it home to Momma but I gues I furgot to giv it to her.

But then my birtday came on Otober tent an my Momma cam home lait after I hed all redy goten home frum scholl. She all ways cum home lait cause she wuks clening ritch folks homes all day. But this time she hed this whit rabbit in this box with hols in it and a pink ribon a round the box and a nother pink ribon a round the rabits neck.

"I brougt you a burthday presunt" she say. "Its a rabit an it will be a tes for you to cee if you can lurn to be sponsable an care for an animal of yur own. We'll call it the rabbit test."

"Don' be givin me no rabbit Momma. I'se bad fo rabbits."

"What you talkin bout, chile?"

"They dun giv me a rabbit tes in scholl las munth an tole me the rabit dyed. I ain good fo rabits I reckon."

THE END

Epilogue

On January 16, 1999 the *Beaufort Gazette* reported that in the year 1997 over 40 high-school girls, and seven girls in middle schools (6th - 8th grade), in Beaufort County became pregnant. And that's a fact. You can look it up.

Bitches on the Beach

Someone once asked me to write a story about "a girl, a dog, and the beach." It is interesting that these very things had an important place in my own life. A turning point, you might say.

To begin with, I was supposed to be a boy. Before I was born my parents had already chosen my name - George - which they didn't bother to change when I turned out, or came out, a girl. I was an only child, but had some cousins, boy cousins, mostly older, that I used to play with. Actually, when I was growing up, I liked doing "boy things" more than girl things. I would rather climb trees or throw stones or make airplanes than play with dolls and tea sets.

But still, I hated my name, George. That is, until I got to High School and learned I wasn't the only woman in the world who lived with the name George. There were George Sand and George Eliot, who became idols for me.

Anyway, the story begins with the weekend of my eighteenth birthday. I was out of school but still living at home with Mom and Socrates, our golden retriever. Dad had just come back from one of the many wars he was always fighting in - he was a Colonel in the Army, Armored Corps, and a West Point graduate. So the three of us decided on a week of togetherness at Bethany Beach, Delaware. I took some books and a snorkel mask, looking forward to some time by myself after a busy school year.

Dad and I used to be very close, and after being away so long he wanted to know all about me and my thoughts and what I had been doing. He seemed especially interested in the boys I knew, and he wanted to know who I had been dating and all that. I think he was surprised and maybe disappointed to learn that I didn't have a "boy friend," wasn't "dating" anyone, and certainly hadn't "done" anything. If the truth be known, I wasn't very interested in boys. I think I had outgrown them; they all seemed to be getting more and more juvenile and gauche as they got older, while I, of course, was getting smarter and wiser. The boys I knew in high school were all a bunch of clods.

At the beach the next morning Mom had been up early and out with the dog. She came in saying she had seen someone on the beach, in the distance, with another golden retriever that looked like Socrates. She said she didn't get close but that whoever it was was wearing black trousers and had a nice walk. Mom also bore the news that a sign at the end of the street said no dogs allowed on the beach 7:30 a.m. until 9:30 p.m. That meant you could take your dog to the beach if you got up early.

Dad had come down and heard enough to say I should take Socrates to the beach early the next day, reminding me with a chuckle that he and Mom had first met on the beach at Nantucket twenty-one, or was it twenty-two, years ago. All right, I said, sure. I'll do it.

So Socrates and I went to the beach the next morning. And the morning after that. And every morning for the rest of the week. And of course we met the other golden retriever; his name was Rex (Good Grief!) And we met his owner, in the black trousers, who was about three years older than I, and studying business in graduate school. We hit it off very well. There were a lot of things we liked in common besides dogs, and that included snorkeling and SCUBA diving, and gardening, and good wine, and good books, especially nineteenth century classics (including "the Georges").

My parents, Dad especially, were delighted when I told them I thought I had found a friend I really liked, Rex's owner. And I was sorry when our week at the beach came to an end, but my new friend and I promised to see each other when we got back to the city. And we did, quite often in fact. The truth is, I had fallen in love.

Mom and Dad lived in a small house, not big enough to have visitors come to spend the night, but didn't mind if I went off to visit someone else. After all, I was a big girl now. I was eighteen, almost eighteen and a half, and I had a job and it was time I moved out anyway. So one day I sort of popped a question. "How would you feel if I went off and lived with someone . . . ? I mean, lived with my friend?

My parents were rather old-fashioned and I wasn't sure how they would react. Mom thought it would be "okay." Dad thought we should be married or at least engaged before living together.

"Dad," I said, "this isn't Canada! Or even Massachusetts or Vermont. This is Delaware."

THE END

Epilogue

The name of Rex's owner who wore the black trousers was, and is, Mary Grace, and we have been together for almost ten years. She is a successful CPA with her own accounting firm, and I am her office manager. We are now happily living in a suburban area of eastern Massachusetts. We have two daughters, three and six, whom we adopted from China two years ago. (In China they only put up girl babies for adoption.) I still love going to the beach and adding to my memories of sand, and Socrates, and Mary Grace in her black trousers. Now we go to one of the beaches on the North Shore, or Cape Cod. We don't go to the beach in Delaware anymore. The last time we were there someone had doctored up the sign so that it read, "No dogs or Lesbian bitches . . . "

Hello There!

I'm a pretty ordinary guy, but sometimes things happen even to ordinary people.

Take for instance that dinner at Duke Zeibert's Restaurant on K Street. It was a quiet, mid-week evening, and the first time I had ever eaten there - but I am getting ahead of myself . . .

I started to tell you that statistically my life must be as ordinary as that of the non-existent "average American" who is always mentioned in surveys and in the news. I'm 38, a college graduate, married eleven years, two children, love my family, and like my job as an actuarial analyst working for a big insurance company.

My wife is smarter than I am in most things, I'll admit it. And her parents were big-time socialites in Washington, so although I'm sure she loves me in her way, she has always made me feel that she did me a big favor in stepping down to my level to marry me.

Except for some of the girls we fooled around with in high school, there is only one other woman in my life that I have ever, shall we say, been intimate with. But being the first, she has always remained very special to me. Anna-Madeleine was her name. Anna-Madeleine Petrowska, a coal-miner's daughter from Pennsylvania that I knew and dated in college. Marriage for us was out of the question; politically we were from opposite poles (so to speak) and our religious differences posed an insurmountable obstacle, but the physical chemistry, as it has been called, was unequaled. I was always comfortable just being with her, but it was our romantic activities that were supreme. Even after I got married, Anna-Madeleine and I continued to see each other occasionally. She was a part of my life with a deep root.

Our meetings were always very quiet and discreet, usually mid-day and mid-week in some out-of-the-way place. We tacitly agreed never to talk about our spouses (or politics or religion). I didn't know anything about her married life. But we filled a need that each of us had, and over the years we never hurt anybody. We never talked about other people, only about ourselves.

But like I say, I loved my wife. I admired her for her brains and loved her as the center of our family even though she never let me forget that I was somewhat her inferior. She was closer to God than I was. She was purer than I. She was more discriminating than I, and had better taste and judgment than I did. Sometimes she made me feel a little put-down - in truth she kept me in my place - but nevertheless I really admired her and looked up to her.

This state of affairs went on for some years, and then the unimaginable, the inconceivable, the impossible, suddenly proved to be possible and imaginable, and indeed, true. Yes, true. My wife was having an affair. The initial evidence was scanty, and came as such a surprise to me that at first I did not believe it. But some research revealed the incontrovertible fact that she had been regularly seeing another man, afternoons, when I thought she was teaching as a substitute at the high school. I was appalled. Can you imagine Doris Day cheating on her husband? I then learned through devious methods that the man worked for the same insurance company that I did; he was Regional Director for the Baltimore Area. I had heard of him, but in the big corporation had never met him.

Inwardly I thought what poor taste my wife showed on this one. Good Grief! The same insurance company? At least she could have gone outside the organization.

And then I began to think. Is my marriage being threatened? Should I confront her? Or should I ignore the whole thing and hope he goes away? Could I use my new knowledge in some meaningful manner? I began to think of the times my wife had put me down, criticizing me in front of people for forgetting to pull out her chair at dinner, for putting my feet up on the arm of the couch, for leaving my button-down shirt collar unbuttoned, for watching football on TV while she preferred her beloved opera. And how she always used to make a point of quietly apologizing all around to her society friends for my inability to tie a black bow tie and my need to rely upon the clip-on variety. All little things, but little things add up.

And, thinking of all these little things which fed her smug superiority, I began to imagine how sweet it would be to redress the balance, and I realized that this was quite an opportunity that had dropped into my lap. Yes. And I would take advantage of it. I would not tell her I knew; I would draw it out, savor it, make her wonder, make her sweat a bit, see how she reacts to insecurity and doubt and innuendo about her own behavior. I relished the thought of perhaps even getting to the same level with her for a change. Even bring her level down to mine if I could not bring mine up to hers. I was tired of being looked down upon, all these years.

So I began to plan.

I had been with the Company for a quite a while and had some pretty good connections. With some effort I arranged to set up a dinner meeting with the Regional Director for the Baltimore Area, having cooked up some matters which I insisted were of mutual interest. As I had never met him, he favored a business luncheon, but I held out for an evening dinner with our wives included, saying that a woman's view on some of these matters could be useful. We agreed to meet at Duke Zeibert's Restaurant on K Street at eight p.m. the following Thursday.

And, oh my! Those three days prior to our dinner meeting! How I did relish them! Of course I did not tell my wife who we were going to have dinner with; she had been out with me for business suppers in the past and was ready to take this one in stride. She loved dominating the social scene, commanding the conversation, talking to the waiters in French, commenting on the vintage of the wine, and generally being the snob that comes so easily to her.

But this time, wouldn't I enjoy watching her face when she sees her lover at the dinner table and tries to make small talk in front of HIM! Let me see how she calls upon her social graces this time! I would watch her squirm; I would drop a few innuendos suggesting that perhaps - only perhaps - I knew something had been going on between them. I pictured my wife at a loss for words, a condition which until now was unheard of. A new first.

And at home after the dinner I could ask her how she liked it, and what she thought of HIM. Oh, yes! I would rub it in. Gently, gently. Rub it in. Deep. I would fix her, I would! Yes, I would take her down a peg or two.

So you can imagine my excitement and eager anticipation when we went into Duke Zeibert's Restaurant that Thursday evening.

The maître d' said our party had already arrived and showed us to our table. There he was, alone, and I thought we had agreed to bring the women. With his slick black hair and three-piece pin-stripe suit, he looked like an insurance salesman in full control of the world. But when he saw my wife, the wide smile across his face suddenly froze into white marble. Oh, I was going to enjoy this! "Hello, I'm John," he managed to say.

At that moment a woman came back from the ladies' room. John stammered, "I'd like you to meet my wife, Anna-Madeleine."

"Oh shit," I muttered, under my breath, as my face went white.

THE END

Playing It Cool

Ever since the evening I first met Belinda I knew I wanted her. It was a routine dinner party with mutual friends, at a table with several other lovely people and lively conversation, which I neither saw nor heard. Belinda, sitting next to me, captivated me from the moment I set eyes on her, and I have no recollection of any of the others present.

Belinda's voice was like music; her eyes had the deep look of a window into another world that is the stuff and substance poets live on; her neck fitted into her shoulders oh so neatly. Never before had I noticed what perfection there could be in the way a woman's neck fitted into her shoulders. Dropping a little lower, her twin treasures rested gently in soft support, modest but suggestive in the symmetry of their contour. Her entire body, as much as I could see of it, conformed to - nay, defined - my image of the ideal woman's physical attributes, gentle but firm.

Her voice also was gentle but firm, obviously directed by a thoughtful mind. I loved listening to her, to her ideas, thoughts, and feelings, and sharing my thoughts and feelings with her. I sensed an undertone of harmonious vibrations, and I felt that, as my children would have said, we clicked.

I had been married before, twice, and had had a few affairs in addition. So I think I knew I was looking at something good.

But getting on with my story. I got her name and phone number, called her the next day, and took her out to dinner the following Saturday.

By now my libido was bubbling over, but this was some special person, you know, high class, and I didn't want to spoil things by coming on too fast. I tried to cast myself in the mold of a solid, sincere type who loved her for her mind and her character, making it clear that I wasn't one of those men who "only want one thing," much as I did want it. But wow . . . ! did I ever want it! Need it. Had to have it. Bad. It had been some months since my last girl friend left me with no other explanation than that she was getting too old for so much childish physical activity. I was, quite frankly, as Harold Robbins would say, extremely horny. But I also had visions of Belinda and me possibly developing some sort of long-term relationship, something more than the immediate gratification my overwrought body now craved so intensely. Play it cool, I told myself. Don't mess up now and scare her away. Even though there was fire raging in the furnace there was also the possibility of nascent love beating in the heart. Maybe even true love.

I saw Belinda several times in the month that followed, usually taking her to a restaurant or bistro for a cozy dinner for two, or an occasional show; once we drove several hours into the country to spend the weekend visiting friends of mine and friends of hers who lived near each other and who, as it turned out, served as convenient chaperons. I was still afraid of scaring Belinda off if she thought (or found out) all I really wanted was sex.

At the end of the month my job took me far away. I wrote to her fairly regularly without, I thought, being too suggestive or blatant in proffering my love, never actually mentioning that powerful word. I did send her some flowers and a few of my old poems and a collection of pictures from my new surroundings. She responded with occasional phone calls, always delightfully sparkling and fresh, and always filled with cheery news of her activities - she taught school, played in the village band, spent time gardening, reading, and visiting with her family. All things I also love and can relate to.

So I began to feel closer to her than ever, even though there were miles between us, and I began to try and think of something that would actually put us together. I told her I would like to invite her for a week or two on a Mediterranean cruise ship sometime soon, or a visit to a place I knew on the beach in Yucatan.

I dreamed on - it would be . . . oh so nice . . . ! And after some champagne at the Captain's Table we would go back to our cozy stateroom, and we would gently, naturally, slip into the ineffable joy that is only at its best when two people are in love and are so ideally suited to each other as Belinda and I were.

Then the shock came.

In those days I was still subscribing to the same newspaper that Belinda got; I liked the idea of reading the same words I knew she was reading. One day I was perusing the "Personals" column - out of curiosity, you understand. I felt it was sad that there were so many people who did not have someone special to care for or think about.

Well, I saw a telephone number that looked familiar.

Holy Cow! Belinda's number! But it can't be real. It's a mistake. A digit or two out of place. I called Belinda to tell her of the funny thing I saw - the misprint in the Personals column giving her telephone number. We would have a good laugh.

"What's so funny about that?" she said.

"What . . . ! Do you mean . . . ?"

"I mean I put in an ad for 'a little light romantic adventure,' nothing serious. What's wrong with that?"

"But . . . Belinda . . . " I babbled . . . "I love you!" It was the first time I had ever actually said it.

"Yes, I know."

"You knew that? And you still . . . ?"

"And I am very fond of you too, but I don't want to get too deeply involved with men again. I've been that route."

"But . . . but . . . ! We don't have to get involved. We can just . . . I mean, if it's romance you want that's fine with me. It's what I want too! It's what I've always wanted, ever since I first met you."

"No," she said, "you want more, and I'm afraid it might lead to deeper involvement. And I never want to get that involved again. Excuse me, I have an incoming call on the line."

"Waaaah . . . !"

And that was that.

THE END

Making Arrangements

A lot of people will tell you that they are middle-of-the-road politically, and that they take a balanced view of things, whether it is true or not. But I really am, and I really do. The other members of my family are all poles apart, so it is a good thing you came to me to learn the truth about how things are with us.

To begin with, I don't know how Mom and Dad were able to survive twenty-nine years of marriage with so few arguments, considering that she has always clung to her feminist stance ever since I can remember, while Dad is pretty opinionated, and even somewhat bigoted and reactionary, although he would never openly acknowledge it. For instance, he will tell you he is in favor of environmental conservation, and equal civil rights for minorities and women and all that, although when he inherited some woodland from his uncle before I was born he promptly sold it off for a housing development to make as much profit as he could. And I bet he would flip if they ever admitted a Negro, or a colored man as he called them, to the City Club, his beloved men's club downtown. He almost resigned five years ago when the first Catholics got in as members, although he wouldn't admit it now.

But he will admit that he went to Harvard. In fact, he never forgets it, and won't let anyone else forget it either. This story is partly about that and partly about my younger sister, Jean. Jean is just as far left-wing as Mom, and even in high school she was always joining peace marches or writing letters about equal pay for women and minorities and so forth. She graduated from college three years ago and now has a good job with a book publishing firm in New Haven. Fortunately she is close enough to drive to our parents' home in Gloucester for dinner once every month or so, and of course my wife and I always join them, as we live in nearby Boston.

Once or twice Jean has brought along a special friend that she had been dating or something. However, our family dinners did nothing to help her relationships. Dad never found any of her friends sufficiently to his taste to refrain from raking them over the coals because they supported the UN or Greenpeace, or were pro-choice or something. But he was always rather subtle about it at the same time. He never actually said that he opposed these things, but merely that he was distressed by people who ignored "family values" and whose morals and patriotism had "gone to the dogs." Things like that. He used to say that if people wanted to live in America they should "act like Americans," but, being his only son and having grown up in his household, I knew what he really meant.

Anyway, I think Dad drove off a lot of my sister's potential boyfriends, and so I was especially interested last week when she announced that she had another friend she wanted all of us to meet. This one was very special, she said. She was thinking of getting engaged.

"Where did you meet him? What's he like?" Dad immediately wanted to know.

"Dad," she said, "before I answer that, I want you to know that I love him very much; he is the one I want to marry. I also want you to remember how many times you have said you were broad minded and how important it was for me to make my own decisions."

"What's all this leading up to, anyway?" Dad retorted.

"There are some things about him you may not like. But to answer your questions, I met him at Yale and I. . . "

"What! At Yale? How many times have I told you never to touch a Yalie? My dear, this is unacceptable. Absolutely unacceptable. I will never have a Yalie darken my door, let alone have my daughter's hand in marriage. Anything but that! I can accept any ethnic grouping, any religion, even Catholic, any - I was going to say sex, but I won't go that far - any linguistic, cultural, or social minority as long as it's a man, but not a Yalie! No, never! Don't ask that of me! There are plenty of other men out there that are not Yalies. Go find one of them!"

"Dad, he is not a Yalie. He is in Yale Law School, and he's going to be a good lawyer. He has the most remarkable powers of persuasion; he can take any side of any issue and make you believe he is right. But in actual fact he is a Harvard graduate, just like you."

Dad of course had a sudden turnabout. His face lost its scarlet fury, and his eyes slowly retreated back into their sockets as he began to cool down a bit. "Okay," he said, "bring him on. Let's have a look at him."

"Dad," continued my sister, "I'm glad you said what you did about all the things you can accept in a son-in-law. You really are broad minded down deep, and I do love you for it."

"Thank you, my precious one. Your love is dear to me and anyone you love I shall love too . . . as long as he is not a Yalie!"

"Well, he's not a Yalie. He was born and raised in South Africa, but is now a US citizen studying law."

What she didn't tell Dad then was that he was a member of an ethnic and racial minority which constituted the majority in that country. So at our family dinner the following Saturday, my sister arrived with her black boyfriend. As they came in the door, she tried to introduce him to Mom and Dad, but Dad heard nothing. He was speechless before the tall black man standing in the hallway with my sister. "This is Charlie," she repeated.

How we got to the supper table, I do not know. It all reminded me of the movie "Look Who's Coming for Dinner," with Sidney Poitier. I think Dad was honestly surprised that the fellow could speak English - the King's English at that - and that his table manners included knowing how to hold his knife, and which fork to use for the salad. I don't remember the feeble attempts at conversation that went around the table, but I do remember that much of it consisted of silence. Charlie was cool but polite throughout. After dinner Dad got up and declared that he and Charlie were going into the library for a little discussion.

The four of us - my wife was with us of course - could not refrain from all sorts of conjectures regarding the agony to which my father was doubtlessly subjecting Charlie, and we would not have been surprised to see the fellow stagger out, bleeding profusely from his eyes, ears, nose, and throat. But when they did emerge half an hour later, I could hardly believe what I saw: Dad was all smiles. With his arm around the young man's shoulder, he started in:

"Charlie Thompson is a fine young man. He understands what a crime against God abortion and stem-cell research are, and he appreciates the importance of having our military interrogate suspected terrorists with the most effective techniques possible. Furthermore," Dad continued, "he adheres to our cherished family values including respect for the flag and the right of the homeowner to bear arms. He'll be a lawyer before you know it, and then he wants ultimately to be a Supreme Court Justice. And he would be a good one. He's exactly the kind of man we need up there on that bench.

"We'll have the wedding reception at the City Club . . . I'll make the arrangements."

THE END

That's Okay

There are some things about romance that I don't understand. And I'm not saying that just to be funny. I mean, for instance, that when a guy and a girl know each other, or even when they are going together, it always seems that one of them cares for the other more, or even loves the other one more, than the other loves him or her.

And I am not even sure which one it is preferable to be, the one who *gives* most of the loving and attention or the one who *receives* most of the attention.

I think most people I know would rather BE loved, even if they didn't love back to the same degree. However, that has not always been the case with me, as this story will tell.

To begin with, I first fell in love - or thought I did, which is the same thing - in high school, but the object of my affection would hardly ever notice me or give me the time of day, and shortly after graduation married the class valedictorian and editor of our school newspaper.

I went on to college, and after I graduated and had a good job I got married too, to someone, who like my high-school sweetheart, I loved more than they loved me. For me it was a happy marriage, but after six years it ended abruptly in divorce, when it came out that my darling spouse had been having an affair with someone else.

I had been single for about three years, without finding anybody particularly special, until last spring when I ran into my old high-school sweetheart who had also been divorced but was about to leave on an assignment with the Peace Corps in Upper Volta, if you know where that is. I was both excited to feel the old feeling stirring up in me, and sad not to be able to pursue it right away because of this Peace Corps thing. Anyway, we had a few hugs and one or two kisses at the airport, and promised to write and to see each other after the affairs of Ouagadougou were settled. I was happy again, with something, and someone, to look forward to.

But the weeks passed slowly. Mail to and from Upper Volta took an eternity: two to three weeks each way, making a month or six weeks for an exchange of letters. This was all before the days of e-mail, of course.

I was "faithful" for a while - several months in fact - but I wasn't born to be celibate forever. And then one weekend at a college reunion I met Leigh, who had been in my class. In those days we had known each other only slightly, and neither of us had ever felt any particular interest in the other. Leigh had never married but was a successful poet and editor of a fashion magazine.

Anyway, we had some pretty hot parties at this reunion, and Leigh and I got to drinking and talking and telling lies about the old days and the parties after the football games when the routine at the dorm was to see how many "sea-breezes" you could drink and still stand up. Sea-breezes, basically gin and grapefruit juice, were the cheapest way we knew of to get tight as fast as possible. And I do confess they still tasted pretty good, and besides, you can drink a lot more of them than you can martinis. Anyway, Leigh and I got tight talking about old times, and drinking toasts to old times, and fooling around, and then we got horny, and then we went and spent the next two days in the sack, you know, making out, multiple moments. It was something I must have been craving more than I realized, but when I sobered up Monday afternoon and looked around, it didn't take me long to realize I had made a big mistake.

Leigh was bright and talkative and chipper and full of non-sequiturs and nonsensical chatter, about loving me and wanting to get married and have children and buy a big house - the whole nine yards. I dressed, mumbled goodbye, slipped out and went back to my two-room apartment.

But I didn't get off that easily, and the next ten days were agony.

I don't know if you have ever had someone calling you up every day, and writing letters to you every day with tender messages of love and mush, but believe me, is does get boring soon. That is, of course, if you don't love them back. And I didn't. I was being inundated with offers of cozy dinners, weekends in a mountain lodge, even a one-week Caribbean cruise out of Fort Lauderdale. Now all that may sound inviting to you, but to me it sounded like a Devil's quagmire, trying to suck me down - down, down, into a tangled mess, trying to destroy my individuality, my freedom, my self-respect, me.

I had to figure some way out of it all. Had to. So I thought and thought and I finally had an idea. It would be harsh and cruel, it is true, but I had to do something to end this nightmare, short of outright murder.

So the next time I met Leigh I fabricated a story and started in, saying we can't have children, we can't get married, we can't see each other anymore. It is what's best. Best for you.

"But why? Why not? Why are you saying such things?"

"It's because . . . " I hesitated a bit for effect . . . "It's because I may have AIDS. I'm HIV positive."

I confess I felt a certain pity or qualm of conscience for coming down so hard with such a blatant lie. But I was glad to get it out and get it over with and be free again at last. That is, for a second or two, until Leigh replied: "Oh, that's okay, Darling. So am I."

THE END

Anything You Want

"How are you feeling, Son?" The words sounded muffled and distant, as though they were coming through a foggy cloud, from another world. "Can you hear me, Son? How are you feeling?" The man's voice droned on, insisting. I tried to concentrate. Someone was talking to me as I lay there. Where was I? What was going on?

My head was pounding, my eyeballs were on fire, whether I moved them or not. My body ached from head to toe with a persuasive, constant pain. I moved my eyes a little. It hurt. Hurt bad. I tried moving a leg, but couldn't do it. My legs seemed locked in a vise of searing pain that shot like electricity right up through my hips and stomach and my backbone.

Sleep. Oh dear God, let me go back to sleep. Maybe the next time I wake up I will find this is all a dream. A nightmare, rather.

"His eyelids are fluttering," said a woman's voice; "I think he is regaining consciousness." She must have touched my hand with hers. It felt cool and human, as though life were flowing from it to me, for a minute there.

With great effort and in spite of the pain, I slowly raised my eyelids and saw two misty figures in white, standing by my bed, one with a black cord that looked like a snake around his neck. I knew enough to realize it was a stethoscope. A doctor. The stethoscope is of course the badge of a doctor; doctors wear it whether they need it or not.

I knew about stethoscopes, and the smell of ether and formaldehyde; I was a medic in the Army, or had been up to then. I let my eyelids gently close themselves again, and as I slowly continued coming to I tried to reconstruct events in my mind.

I remember joining the Army right out of high school. My father pushed for it, insisting it was the patriotic thing to do. He also went on about the wide range of training opportunities the Army offers, and how it could help me learn a trade and make a man of me. I had been a fairly good student, mostly A's and B's, and a fairly good athlete - I had run a mile in 4:39, tying the high school record.

I would have liked to study medicine and become a doctor, but neither my brains nor my brawn had been quite good enough to get me a scholarship in a good college, and there was no money for anything like higher education in our family. What was left over after rent and food and clothes for my younger brothers and sisters must have gone for my father's booze and lottery tickets. Lottery tickets are supposed to provide funds for the State education program. Is that irony, or what?

So six years later I was still serving in the Army as a medic driving an ambulance in the war. Front lines. How I got from there to this bed of pain with two ghost-like figures in white standing over me was not exactly clear to me.

I do remember the fighting had been severe. For several weeks our positions had been receiving constantly increasing mortar and rocket fire from the enemy. Our casualties were mounting. To say that war is hell is to say nothing. No one who has not been in it can imagine what it is like there in the mud and the heat with the weariness and the hunger. And the stink. Oh, God, the stink of rotting human flesh and dead body wastes. And the pitiful cries of dying men, followed by an even more pitiful silence. No one who has not been there can imagine what it is like to see the staring eyes of a man who yesterday was your comrade, eyes coming out of the front half of a skull whose back half had been blown open leaving a gaping hole wet with liquid brains oozing out, down his neck onto his shoulders. But we medics had to focus on the living, the lucky ones, with mutilated arms, legs, and bodies. It was all in a day's work for us as we slogged away, trying to ease the pain and give as much medical attention as possible before getting them to a field hospital farther back behind the lines.

But I never thought it would happen to me.

I must have hit a land mine. Probably one of our own. I remember I was alone at the time, driving across a field to detour around a giant bomb crater when there came an explosion that lifted the vehicle right off the ground and seemed to be the end of everything. Flying shrapnel and twisted metal parts everywhere. I knew I had been hurt, but didn't feel any pain. Not at first. However, I could hardly move my arms and couldn't move my legs at all. Strange thoughts ran through my mind. How will I drive back if my legs won't move? The vehicle was in ruins but I was still in it and in my state of shock I could only think that I had to go on driving it - go on with my job. Then the pain took over. A dull aching pain at first, then a searing pain, then a feeling of ice and fire, mixed together, all over me. Then darkness. Blessed darkness. How long that lasted, I do not know. Maybe several days.

"Son, do you hear me?" That voice again. I tried to speak but couldn't. I guess my lips moved, for then the woman said, with a cheery voice, "Look, he's alive! He's going to live." "Do you know where you are?" the man continued. I rolled my head slightly from left to right. No. "You are in the 703rd Division Hospital. You have had a little accident and we are taking care of you. And I have good news for you. Can you hear me?" I nodded perceptibly.

"Good news and some bad news, of course," he said with an encouraging smile.

With great effort I found my tongue and muttered, "I think you'd better give me the good news first."

"The good news is that you are going to live! You're going to live! And there's more good news. The Army has a wide range of prosthetic devices available at no cost. You'll be a Veteran!"

"Prosthetic devices . . . ? You mean my foot was crushed, don't you? I still have pain and strange feeling all the way to my toes. Go on, you can tell me . . . How bad is it?"

"Phantom pains they are, my boy. They're quite common among amputees."

"You mean you amputated my foot? I can't move anything down there. It all hurts."

"Well, no. It wasn't just your foot we had to amputate."

"What are you saying? You mean you amputated my leg? Oh my God!"

"Steady, Son. Many veterans lead busy and useful lives without their legs. And the artificial limbs available nowadays are really superb. Almost as good as the real thing."

"Legs . . . legs? What are you saying?"

"I'm sorry, my Boy. We had to amputate both legs . . . but only one of them above the knee. They were full of gangrene. It was that or your life. But you still have one knee that is perfectly good."

I couldn't respond. A life without legs? One knee? What kind of a life would that be? Better no life at all.

"But there is more good news," he continued. I rolled my eyes back in his direction. "You will be getting a nice pension. You'll probably be getting over nine hundred per. Tax-free."

"Nine hundred per week?" I managed to say.

"Well, no. Nine hundred per month. But it's all tax-free and it will be yours to do anything you want to with it."

I closed my eyes once more.

THE END

Getting Even

Everyone has heard stories of somebody who reappears twenty-five or thirty years later in the image of a parent. Sometimes there is a surprise, for it may turn out that in spite of a superficial family resemblance the prodigal child is not at all like the parent, but in fact is quite a different person underneath.

However, in this story it really was almost as though Jeannie Campbell had returned a generation later and was now the young woman standing in front of me, talking to me, looking at me with those same light brown eyes I had looked into so many years before. I was no longer with a stranger I had just met. I was with Jeannie, someone that I knew, that was close to me, that had been dear to me in the distant past and whom I had never completely forgotten in the intervening decades.

We talked about a million things - anything and everything, just what, I cannot say. And even though it was the first time I had ever met this young woman, I felt we had immediately established a close bond. Or perhaps we merely discovered a mysterious bond that had always existed between us, even before we met, before we ever knew it. It was indeed almost as though she was the Jeannie I had known, and had now returned.

Ignoring the charming company of the others there at Aunt Agnes's cocktail party, the young woman and I let our conversation run on and on, sharing our ideas and feelings about politics, philosophy, family, art and music, education, the environment, and even love and war and peace, finding ourselves drawn ever closer into a certain oneness in the similarity of our views and the harmony of our feelings. Too bad this young woman was so young, I thought - young enough to be my daughter. How could there be such a thoughtful and wise head attached to such a youthful body? It was the same thoughtful and wise mind I had known years before - Jeannie Campbell's mind.

I reveled in the pleasure of her company, in an exciting world half real and half dreamy, but the cocktail hour ticked by all too quickly, and soon it became time to leave the party. Then, just before I left, she said something I will never forget: the six most beautiful words I have ever heard in my life, although I have never told anyone about it. I don't think I COULD have told anyone about it, certainly not Jeannie or George, who I would probably never see again anyway.

Jeannie had been the first woman who ever captivated me and my tender heart. I was a freshman in college and she was a year behind me, still in high-school, but I loved her truly, with a sincere love that (unfortunately) would have met my grandmother's strictest standards of Victorian propriety. Then she went off to college in a different city, and suddenly, before I could connect with her again or arrange to transfer to another university close enough to allow me to resume my pursuit, I learned that she had gotten married. Married, yet. To someone else. Someone else who turned out to be some son-of-a-bitch from Princeton named George.

I was devastated, swamped with successive waves of depression and frustrated fury, and consumed by bitterness from the injustice of it all. Oh, how I would have liked somehow to get even with George - this George fellow who did not even know I existed. But of course it was hopeless. The die was cast, and furthermore I am a cowardly pacifist by nature, certainly not brave enough to seek vindication through violence. I just had to accept it, or forget it, or at least try.

Of course George wasn't really a son-of-a-bitch. From the impression I gathered, probably the worst thing anyone could say about him was that he was something of "a square," as we used to say. Lackluster perhaps, maybe somewhat unimaginative, certainly not dumb but plodding and persevering, good at what he did, a solid citizen who gave to charities, sat on boards of directors of corporations and benevolent associations, knew all the important people in his own town and a lot of unimportant people as well, but few outside it. Never learned a foreign language or traveled much except for occasional insurance meetings or conventions in Chicago or Los Angeles or Hartford. It could hardly fit into my mind, the idea that this was his daughter now in front of me, talking to me. No, it was Jeannie, in some sort of reincarnation. Jeannie, bubbling with youthful vitality. Jeannie, having magically returned.

But when the time for this happy interlude did come to an end, I left Aunt Agnes's cocktail party walking on air, with wings on my feet, a tear of joy in my eye, and a treasure in my heart. My compensation was complete. The six last words this lovely young woman had given me were still ringing and singing in my ears. It was only later that I realized I had my vindication and that I had finally gotten even without even trying.

Her words were, "Oh, why didn't YOU marry Mom?"

THE END

Epilogue

In my mind, for many months, I could still hear the echo of those six little words. And I wondered whether anything in this life ever could have turned out any different than the way it actually DID turn out. In my fancy I even wondered what might happen were I to outlive George and some day meet Jeannie again. Jeannie the mother. Jeannie the grandmother and perhaps the great-grandmother. Jeannie, who by now must be old and bent, and tired and wrinkled. But Jeannie now single, maybe even alone.

Then just last week I learned that George had in fact died a year ago and that Jeannie was now living in a little cabin in the backwoods of Vermont, so remote as to be snowed in most of the winter.

And I began to wonder where I had stored my old snowshoes and whether I would ever be able to find them again.

Hasta La Vista

My name is Patrick L. Bushmill, and I am a Sergeant in the Army Reserves.

When I came back to the USA after serving two years in a war zone overseas, I wanted out. I had had enough. "Hasta la vista, amigo," I said to the mustering-out officer at Fort Devens as I shouldered my pack to head for home.

"What did you say . . . ? What does that mean?" the jerk asked.

"It's Mexican talk. It's like, well, 'Goodbye'," I said. "Toodle-oo. You know - hasta la vista." I could have said "adiós" just as easily, I thought. Don't know why I didn't. Anyway, I was out now and heading for home.

The little town I live in is nothing if it is not patriotic. Our population was only 1,130 at the time of the last census, but on a clear day you could see more flags flying from front yards and backyards and porches and automobile antennas and dog houses than you will ever see in any other town ten times our size. And that's on an ordinary day, not just the Fourth of July. And the Fourth of July - well, you would have to see that to believe it. We must get five or six thousand out there for our parade, and band concert, and fireworks, and that's more people than there ARE in our town. I mean we attract patriots from all over the county, and from some other counties too. After all, the name of our town is Liberty. Liberty, USA. Liberty, New Hampshire, actually. And that's a fact.

The gift shops here make half their income from buttons and tee shirts and patriotic picture postcards with seven different historic US flags, and that's not even counting the Stars and Bars, which you can also buy if you want, but which as you can imagine is not too popular in New Hampshire. But New Hampshire-ites love their country just as much, and love war just as much, as anybody anywhere in the USA; at least we love the image of patriotically marching off to war with the band playing and the flags flying even if we don't always like what we find when we actually get into war. I mean, as individuals in real battle conditions.

So when my country went to war, Liberty New Hampshire supplied our fair share of volunteers in keeping with our tradition of duty, honor, and country, and I too was one of the volunteers as I couldn't just watch my buddies go while I stayed at home.

It was kind of fun at first; I actually liked the routine and the camaraderie we had in our basic military training. I had always enjoyed the out-of-doors and had led an active life, and at our boot camp, as it was called, I thought it was fun running over the obstacle course and hiking through the woods at night with the other guys, and shooting some nifty new rifles and then taking them all apart and putting them back together. Blindfolded, yet. And swimming with all your clothes on. And even doing the push-ups. And as I had come from Liberty, New Hampshire, I especially liked the weekly parades in honor of every graduating class, complete with a first-rate marching band playing snappy martial music by John Phillip Sousa - a lot better band than the one we had back in Liberty, New Hampshire I might add.

At first we got lots of letters from family and friends at home, since phone calls were discouraged by the management as being too distracting. We answered back with glowing accounts, and even exaggerations, of how much fun we were having.

Then we finished our training and promptly went overseas, right into the thick of the fighting. And things were suddenly different. Very, very different. We had been led to believe we were prepared for everything and could handle any situation under any conditions. The truth is that when we actually got into the fighting it wasn't anything like what we had been led to expect, or what we had been trained to face. Without going into the gory details in this story, I will simply state that war is one hellacious situation after another, and it seemed we rarely even knew where we were or what we should be doing besides trying to stay alive. That went on for two years. I was supposed to be there for eighteen months but they extended my tour because they said they were short of troops. And I could see why they said they were short of troops, with a lot of my comrades around me being wounded - or "mutilated," as the French say - and quite a few being killed as well.

So when I was finally sent back to the States and given a chance to re-enlist for another tour, I respectfully declined. "Hasta la vista, U.S. Army," is what I said. Goodbye is what I meant, in case you don't know Spanish. I never wanted to see the Army again. Anyway, I was out now and heading for home.

At first glance, home hadn't changed much. The house was the same, and Mom and Dad were still there, only three years older. And I was even able to get my old job back at the print shop. But still there was something different in the air that spring, a change in the atmosphere. Or maybe it was just me. But it seemed people were a little more - well, serious - about war and such than they had been before. The list of war casualties that was kept between the flags in front of the City Hall was growing, and when the Fourth of July came, the parade was a much more somber affair than what I had remembered.

And another thing. It was about then that our government decided to bring back the draft and started issuing draft cards, because just relying on volunteers and extending the tours of soldiers already serving had not sufficed to fill the need for troops on the ground. There weren't many volunteers anymore. Instead of volunteering, the new crop of eighteen-year-olds, mostly draftees, were being TOLD what to do - told to go off to war. But there was still something, sort of bothering me, in the back of my head, something that was kind of odd, and strangely annoying. But certainly of no importance, or so I thought. I was glad I had served my time.

I don't know about you, but I don't go in much for psychic stuff and the subconscious and all that, but after I had been home about three months I had a dream where I was surrounded by a dozen or so gypsies, all looking into their crystal balls and wearing Army uniforms except for the turbans they were wearing on their heads. With piercing eyes gazing into the depths of her mystical source of wisdom, one gypsy whispered, "Hasta la vista." Then the next one whispered, a little louder, "Hasta la vista," and the next, and the next, until all around me was a chorus of "Hasta la vista."

And then sudden silence and everything black. I had no idea what it meant. Not then.

But the very next day in the mail I got an official-looking letter with a notice from the U.S. Army reminding me that I was still in the inactive reserves, stating that I was being recalled and telling me to report for duty the first Monday of the following month. I could hardly believe it. It seemed the work of supernatural, psychological, subconscious forces. Supernatural forces among the gypsies; or subconscious forces within me. Maybe I knew all the time that I was going back in. Oh, why hadn't I simply said, "Adiós" instead of "Hasta la vista"? Was it an omen? Or maybe my subconscious felt some premonition I wasn't aware of and made me do it.

THE END

Epilogue

If you want to look it up, you will find that "Hasta la vista" doesn't quite mean "adiós," or "goodbye." It actually means "so long," or "until we meet again." Yuck. This time it was hasta la vista, liberty. Hasta la vista. Or . . . I shuddered . . . or was it really adiós?

Note:
On July 4 of the following year, the hero of this story, Sergeant Patrick L. Bushmill, United States Army Corps of Engineers, was killed in action over there when his jeep hit a land mine on a dirt road that was supposed to have been cleared. He was twenty-three years old. The bomb had been made in the USA; it was one of twenty-

four hundred such land mines we had delivered to a regime we were supporting twenty years earlier, but that regime subsequently turned against us and began to give safe haven to terrorist groups that are intent on doing us harm.

It Wouldn't Be Advisable

Have you ever thought about how luck and circumstances can change a person's life? Take me, for instance. I am basically an honest average guy and a law-abiding citizen, but just how honest I am I didn't realize until quite recently, for all the good it did me. Oh, I've had a few traffic tickets for parking, or for speeding once or twice. Things like that. Back in the days when I had a car. But nothing serious. Probably about the shadiest thing I have ever done was to join in at an illegal crap game downtown a couple of times. Just last week, it was. At first I won a little, almost two hundred dollars. Then I started losing, but I quit while I was still ahead, for I knew that in craps the odds are against you and that in the long run I would lose everything if I kept on. And besides, those guys are pretty tough, and to tell the truth it made me a little nervous just being with them. I am more of a wimp myself, actually.

Anyway, last spring, when the recession hit the hardest, I lost my job, a job I had had for eleven years. Downsizing, the company called it. I was running a machine in a shoe factory, not particularly hard work, but I had dropped out of high-school to take that job when I was seventeen, and I didn't know how to do much of anything else. The result was that, after I was laid off, although I tried, really tried, I couldn't find another job, and five months later I was still unemployed, without a car, almost no money at all, and with my feeble credit worthiness extended to the limit. About the only jobs you heard of were for city garbage men who of course they called sanitary engineers. I was low, but not that low, and I think I would have rather starved than haul garbage cans.

But getting on with my story: I was sitting on a park bench one afternoon when this Luigi character - a guy I had known in high-school - comes up and says straight out, "You look a little shabby; what have you been doing?"

"Nothing much."

"You working?"

"No, not at the moment."

"Maybe I have a job for you. Interested?"

"Depends. Maybe. What's on your mind?"

"All you have to do is spend a little money, just a few dollars."

"Dollars happen to be one thing I'm a little short of right now."

"Not to worry. I'll provide them."

"Go on," I said, "continue."

"You know," he said, "some people don't like to change big bills, like bills over twenty dollars. I have some C-notes that need to be taken down into smaller stuff, like ten's and twenty's. You take a C-note, like, and go buy a little something and you get a bunch of ten's and twenty's in change. It's as simple as that."

"Why don't you just go to a bank and get them to do it?" I asked naively. "That wouldn't be advisable," was the answer.

"Ah, now I see," said I, as the light dawned.

"You can make, like, a hundred dollars a day, and you look as though you need it. You take these three C-notes and make three little purchases, you get the ten's and twenty's in change, you bring them to me, and we split it; you get one third of the take."

My immediate reaction was to tell him in no uncertain terms that I wanted no part of his crooked dealings. But, without thinking, I surprised him, and surprised myself even more, when I heard some unfamiliar corner of my inner psyche respond, "All right, agreed."

Then he peeled off three big bills with Ben Franklin's picture right there on them, and I must admit they looked pretty good. I certainly could never have told they were fake.

"You can't tell them from the real thing," insisted Luigi. "You can mark them with that special ink pen, or hold them up to the light, whatever. They will stand up to any test I know of. In fact, they were made by a guy who used to work for the Bureau of Engraving and Printing. That's the U.S. Mint. And they've got the same ink, the same paper, the same little threads, and the same shiny flakes and spots. All the same. I've got a hundred of these babies," said Luigi, "that's ten thousand dollars. You can make a hundred a day. Three thousand a month. Meet me back here tomorrow at the same time, after you have done your shopping. But three hundred per day is max; we don't want to attract attention by flooding the market."

"Okay," I said, "It's a quarter past twelve. I'll see you back here at a quarter past twelve tomorrow." I took the three bills and started off.

"Just a minute. A few words of advice."

"Yeah? What?"

"Think about where you're going to change your C-notes. You don't go to news-stands and shoe-shine parlors and peanut vendors that deal in nickels and dimes. You go where the money is."

"The money is in the banks."

"Not all of it. And you don't go to foreign currency exchange windows or pawn shops or government surplus stores either. Those guys are suspicious of their own grandmothers. And stay away from banks and post-offices and places like that. They have cameras and x-ray machines and other things you never heard of. Movie houses or theaters are bad too, because, there you are, a sitting duck, should they become suspicious. You have to get in and get out, wherever it is. And I don't need to tell you, never go to the same place twice."

"What's left then?"

"What's left is the stores where the rich people go, especially where the rich foreigners go, to buy expensive clothes and jewelry and art objects and stuff like that. Mostly women. You go in and buy a handkerchief for five or ten dollars and, bingo, you have made ninety or ninety-five dollars. But one other piece of advice: get a haircut and go buy a nice suit at the Salvation Army store. You have to make a good impression if you are going to do this. And do your work at a busy time of day, like in the afternoon or early evening. Don't wait until tomorrow morning. Mornings are less busy and that's not good."

"Okay, okay. I get the idea." And off I went.

Now, I had $82 of my own money in my wallet, left over from selling my car and money I had made in the crap game, and that was about all I had in the world. I took Luigi's advice and found a suit at the Salvation Army store for $24, with coat and pants that almost matched. Then I treated myself to a real meal at a nice restaurant, something I had not done for a good while. After all, I could afford it now with $100 a day coming in regularly, for a month at least. I relaxed with a feeling of euphoria. I felt a sense of accomplishment and satisfaction even though, so far, I hadn't really done anything. But I could now walk with a bounce to my step for the first time in many weeks.

I started to stroll about the shopping streets where the more expensive stores were. And it was true, like Luigi said. Fancy ladies with foreign accents were pulling out big bills from their Italian alligator handbags. Wives of rich drug lords or Mafia types, a lot of them were, I'll bet. I even thought of going back to the crap game. I would have gotten a good deal of inner satisfaction if I could have passed a fake hundred along to one of those thugs, but I soon thought better of it. Those guys would break your knees or break your neck without thinking twice about it if they ever caught you trying to con them like that.

I looked into a lot of store windows, and entered a few doors, looking for the right place. Clerks came up to me, "Can I help you, Sir?"

"No thanks, I am just looking." That went on. TIME went on. But I couldn't bring myself to do the deed. Still, I told myself, I need not worry; it was just that I wasn't used to being in these fancy places. I just needed a little more practice. So I kept on practicing, thinking of the words I would use to buy a handkerchief. But I was still nervous about it, and I began to have self-doubts as my nervousness increased rather than diminished.

Could I really go through with it? How much would it bother my conscience to know that I had been involved in a criminal undertaking? I knew I was a chicken at heart.

I would just have to play a role, like being in a school play. Not think about it. This wasn't really me that would be passing the phony money, but an actor in a make-believe play. That's what I tried telling myself, but it didn't work too well, and my conscience wouldn't buy it. And if I couldn't fool myself, how was I going to be able to fool anyone else into believing I was anything but a chicken?

And so I continued to get more and more nervous, as the psychological thing took hold of me. My palms began to sweat. My temples began to pound. And I still hadn't done anything yet. What would I be like after I had actually done something?

I'll just keep walking some more. The exercise is probably good for me, I thought.

But my nerves were getting more and more worked up all the time. By now it was after 5:00 p.m. and I was nowhere. I should have just gone into the first store I saw and bought something. I was going to have to do it three times and so far I hadn't even done it once. I kept on going for many blocks, for another hour or two, still looking into the windows of all sorts of shops, especially the fancy ones, but my psychological state continued to worsen.

About 7:00 p.m., when it was getting dark and I was almost a nervous wreck, I came to a cinema where an old John Wayne film was playing. Maybe a movie will relax me, I thought. I bought a ticket, paid for it out of my own pocket, and went in and sat down in the back of the theater. I began to review the day's events. At first I didn't feel relaxed at all. I tried to concentrate on the movie, but couldn't. I had no idea what was up there on that screen. All sorts of thoughts were still racing through my mind. What had I gotten myself into? Did I want to be a criminal? What if I got caught? Or even if I didn't get caught, could I live with myself after doing something criminal like this?

I knew what the answer was. The answer was "No." I couldn't go through with it. I just couldn't. Call me weak willed if you want, but the truth is that my spineless nature was telling me it wouldn't be advisable. Tomorrow I would give Luigi back his fake $300 and go find a job with the City Sanitary Engineering Department. They always need garbage-men, and at least I could do that. Yes that is what I would do. A warm sense of comfort came over me. For the first time since noon I began to feel relaxed, as though a load had been lifted from around my neck, and I settled back in my seat. What a relief. Better poor and honest and not having to get the jitters every time I saw a policeman or looked in a mirror. I had learned something about myself, and now I was just going to enjoy the rest of the show that I had paid for. Even if I had to haul garbage cans it would be better than living a life of torment and insecurity.

Then the surprise came, and the next nine hours were a nightmare that you won't believe: something I wish I could forget and simply erase from my life.

It was 4:00 a.m. when they finally let me make a phone call, and luckily I was able to get Luigi on the other end of the line. He wasn't too happy to be disturbed.

"You're not supposed to be calling me," he said. "What the hell is the matter with you?"

"Luigi," I said, trying to be calm, "I need your help."

"What are you talking about? Where are you?"

"I'm in jail. Precinct 27."

"For God's sake! What for? What have you done?"

"They just came and arrested me, like out of the blue."

"You ass! Where'd they get you?"

"At the Majestic Theater, last night. I went to the movies. There was hardly anybody there, and I had only been there half an hour when these two cops came in and grabbed me. Luigi, you have to get me out of here. You don't know what a horrible place a jail is to spend the night in . . . "

"Well, as a matter of fact, I do. I've done that a few times myself."

"Luigi! Please! Get me out of here. They want $10,000 bail money. Come on Luigi, you've got it."

"At the movies? For God's sake! I told you never to try to pass one of them bills in a movie house. You'd be a sitting duck if they ever spotted it."

"But I didn't. I didn't, Luigi! I never passed any of your bills, I swear!"

"Then why in Hell did they arrest you? Did you commit a public nuisance or something?"

"Come on, Luigi, this is no laughing matter. I paid with a ten-dollar bill out of my own pocket. But the cops came into the movie house and grabbed me and frisked me and found the three big bills and wouldn't believe me when I said I was innocent of any wrongdoing. Some son-of-a-bitch at the crap game last week must have paid me with a counterfeit ten-dollar bill, and the ticket-taker called the cops. You have to help me, Luigi! Come on, ten thousand dollars bail money. You've got it. I know you've got it. Luigi? Luigi? Can you hear me?"

His voice became fainter. "I don't think that would be such a good idea. No, it wouldn't be advisable."

THE END

A New Start

How would *you* like to see *your* ex-husband there, practically in front of your face, when you are meeting another man, one you might possibly be getting serious about? Well, it happened to me, and it wasn't much fun. Let me tell you about it.

I still see George, my ex-husband, around town from time to time, and it has never bothered me much. But it was different last week, when I ran into him at the Coffee Cup Café. I definitely did not want to see him there and I foresaw an awkward situation, to say the least. No, I was not at all happy to see him this time, sitting there, as I came into the little tea room where we had sometimes eaten together on previous occasions.

You see, this time I was meeting someone else, a new friend, a new interest, a new man. Maybe even a new relationship. Having George right there wasn't going to help things. No, definitely not.

George and I had been divorced for almost a year, after a marriage of over eighteen years. I was the one who wanted the divorce. At least, I was the one who admitted wanting it. George acted as though he didn't especially care, one way or the other. I didn't have any particular reason, just a lot of little reasons, I guess. Like, our marriage didn't seem to be going anywhere. Like, everything was always the same, the same house in the suburbs, the same tennis partners, the same little old sailboat on weekends, the same old history books that

George so loved to read in the evening and sometimes far into the night. Like, the same old boredom. Like, it was over. Like, coming to the end of a movie. Like, I wanted out. Like, I wanted a new start in life while I was still alive.

George was a little older than I - he had been married before, to a distant cousin of mine, but that only lasted four years. They had a daughter, Wendy, who is now married and living in California. I love Wendy as though she were my own daughter, maybe in part because I had been told I would never have children myself.

When George took an early retirement so we could "do more things together," I thought there might be new hope for our marriage, sort of a new start. We would travel, visit exotic places, study foreign languages, and learn more about opera and the baroque music that we both loved. But his idea of travel was usually a one-week or two-week sailing trip in our boat, along the coast or out to the islands. Not that I didn't like it; I loved the sailboat, just like he did, but I still dreamed of a real cruise on a Norwegian liner in the South Pacific or the eastern Mediterranean from Athens to Cairo. I dreamed of opera in Vienna or Milan; only once had we ever been to a real opera house here, when we saw La Boheme at the Met five or six years ago. "Can't afford Europe on my retired pay," George would say. However, I was quite sure he had money stashed away somewhere, but just wasn't touching it.

And there were other things. After George retired and was around the house all day, he just seemed to be more of a load on me. Or else he was telling me how to do things or trying to take over in the kitchen, baking bread, roasting ducks, making goulash and generally creating a mess. And his books - he would leave them all over the house. Memoirs of Ulysses S. Grant, history of the French Revolution, volumes of encyclopedias he had pulled out and not put back. No matter where I looked, no matter what I did, there was George or his trail.

And I knew that divorce laws in this state covered conjugal property rights that split everything down the middle, regardless of its origin. I would find out how much George really had been stashing away on the side over the years.

But getting on with the story: My life with George wasn't all bad, but it wasn't going anywhere either, and I decided I would be better off to strike out on my own. Get a new start. So I went ahead with it. The divorce was worse than I expected, but I expected it to be. As I predicted, there was internecine struggle over the money, which George insisted he didn't have but I knew he did - and while my lawyer did the best she could (and charged me enough, I might say), she was never able to prove that George owned more than a modest amount in a savings account, a modest vacant lot in Texas, and our modest three-bedroom home with twelve years to go on a modest thirty-year mortgage.

However, I was now free to develop my own personality and interests and, like I said, get a new start.

But after a few months enjoying my sudden freedom, I began to realize I was not cut out to be a hermit or live alone, and my bed did seem awfully cold that winter. My best friend at the time was Betty Jamieson, an old school acquaintance who had also been divorced, but was now remarried. Remarried to a wonderful man she said she met through an ad in the "Personals" column of *Harvard Magazine.*

"I don't believe it," I said, when she first told me how she had met her husband.

"Well, it's true. Nice people need some way to meet each other too, you know. Not everybody is going to meet the man of their dreams at the corner bar. Maybe you ought to have a look yourself."

So she showed me a *Harvard Magazine*. (Her brother had gone to Harvard.) And it was true, there in black and white were nice Jewish boys, and WASPS, and doctors, and "financially secure" retirees looking for friends, pen-pals, acquaintances, lovers, mates, even spouses. Of course, a lot of women had ads in there too, even more than the men, but Betty didn't let that faze her in her enthusiasm.

"I could never answer such an ad, right off the bat like that, cold turkey, to someone I didn't know."

"Then what you should do," said Betty, "is write your own ad, and then you can do the choosing from the among the responses. Here, I'll help you write it up."

So we did it.

"Attractive DWF, forty-ish, well built, well educated, eclectic interests including art, music, sailing, tennis, travel, walks on the beach, and quiet times at home. Seeks financially secure non-smoking gentleman fifties to mid-sixties for friendship, conversation, outings, togetherness, maybe more. HM Box 1492."

It was Betty who insisted on the importance of the "togetherness and maybe more." Now, I'm not a prude and I like those things too, but without being given a push I don't think I could have come out and blatantly said so.

I got about a dozen responses; five of them sounded interesting enough for me to write back. One of them, a gentleman named Henry La Fontaine, and I then got onto E-mail and began swapping messages that way, although of course I didn't use my real name. *Harvard Magazine* provided a forwarding service so you didn't have to give your address either, until you wanted to. And I would never give out my telephone number without a lot of screening first, so I made up a name and called myself Adele in my letters and E-mail to Henry. You have to be careful about these things, you know.

Anyway, Henry and I soon realized we had a lot in common; we held similar political views, we both liked the arts and classical music, good food and wine, and Henry had played tennis in an Ivy League college, although I don't think he ever said which one - and he had also done some sailing over the years - all things I like to do too. But I was still cautious about giving out my phone number, and so I never talked to Henry on the telephone. I preferred E-mail, frankly. That way I could think a bit about what I was saying, and see what I had said before I actually said it. That went on for several days, and I was really beginning to feel an attraction for this Henry La Fontaine fellow. So we decided it was time to meet. He wanted to invite me to lunch, and I suggested the Coffee Cup Café because I had eaten there before and thought I would feel less nervous in familiar surroundings. We agreed to meet at 1 p.m. on Thursday. The Coffee Cup Café was a little place, and Thursdays were slow days, so I figured I would have no trouble spotting Henry. But he said he would wear a tweed jacket and a red tie just to be sure. I was now quite excited and looking forward to meeting this man whom I felt I had already begun to know and like quite a lot. I won't go so far as to say that I was falling in love with him, sight unseen, but I do know I was feeling some pretty strong emotion for him already. Maybe he could even become a big part of my future life.

After I parked the car and was walking toward the café a horrible thought struck me. As I said before, George and I had eaten there several times in the past, and I knew he liked the place and probably still ate there sometimes. Well, I certainly hope he's not having lunch there today, I thought. Yes, that would be rather awkward.

And so, when I went into the restaurant at five minutes to one, I suddenly saw that my worst fears were well founded. There were only four tables with customers, but, dammit, there was George, alone at a side table, calmly reading the newspaper, sipping a glass of wine like he owned the world, and now frowning at me over the top of his rimless eyeglasses.

Yes, this is going to be awkward, I thought. My immediate impulse was to do an about face and scoot on out of there, but of course I couldn't do that. I'll just have to ignore him. I have to wait for Henry. He'll be here in a minute; maybe then we can go somewhere else. I'll sit here by the door and catch him as he comes in. I'm sure I'll recognize him in his tweed jacket and red tie.

Business was slow that day. I sat, watching the door, but only one or two couples came in or out. The café was quiet. I didn't have to talk very loud for George to hear me. So after a few minutes I said to him, in a low voice, "What are you doing here?"

"I'm having lunch; what does it look like I'm doing?"

"Are you meeting someone?" I asked, as frightening thoughts of impossible possibilities began gnawing at the edge of my fairy-tale dream world.

"Yes, as a matter of fact, I am, not that it's any business of yours. What are YOU doing . . . ?"

Before I could answer, a tall attractive woman came in and paused, as though she were looking for someone. George stood up from his table and came up to her. "Excuse me," he said, "you must be Adele."

I caught my breath. Holy Cow, I thought. What is this? Did I hear him right? Can there be another Adele? This is strange. I didn't know Adele was that common a name.

"No," said the lady, "I'm Monica Petrowska. So I guess you're not Martin van der Meer. He was supposed to be wearing a green tie; yours is red." George sat down, looking a little puzzled and not so sure of himself as before.

"What did you call her?"

"I thought she was Adele."

The gray clouds of reality were coming nearer, closing in on me.

I took another look at him. It was true. He did have on a red tie, like she said. And, oh oh, tweed jacket. George had never worn a red tie in his life, all the years I had known him. Hardly ever wore any tie, for that matter. I didn't even know he owned a red tie. But there it was. Oh shit. What a son-of-a-bitch.

"Why are you wearing a red tie?" I said, with an heroic effort to control my frustrated fury.

"I like red ties."

"No you don't. You are a lying son-of-a-bitch. You don't like neckties and you hate red. Why don't you go put on a green one?"

"Calm down. What are you talking about?"

"What I am talking about is that you are a lying son-of-a-bitch, that's what I'm talking about. You are not just lying about your necktie, but I'll bet you have been lying to people all over the country, telling them your name is Henry La Fontaine, you son-of-a-bitch!"

"You know about that?"

"Yes, I know about that. And I have been getting your E-mail, in case you hadn't guessed. You've been lying to me about your name, and I don't know what else. Your name isn't Henry. Or IS it Henry and you were lying to me for eighteen years when I thought your name was George?"

"Oh, shit," said George.

"Yes, oh shit," said I.

At least we seemed to agree on that point.

I gathered up my gloves and my handbag at the table and was starting to leave, still appalled at George's atrocious behavior, when he said,

"Goodbye, Adele." His voice sounded somewhat different than usual, not angry, but maybe a little sad.

I hesitated slightly. "Goodbye, Henry . . . Goodbye . . . I guess."

THE END

The Prodigal Calf

Have you ever noticed that life can be happy and joyful sometimes, but sad and ominous at other times? Sometimes, which one it is may depend on the point of view of the observer. I mean, what may be happy to one person having one point of view may be very sad from another point of view, and vice versa. I'll explain what I mean.

To begin with, the other point of view I was thinking of in this case was not that of a human being, but of an animal being. The animal being, being me. I'm not insulting her to say that Mother was a fat cow and that Father was as strong as a bull. He WAS a bull, and still is in fact, and my mother is still a cow. And I am still a calf, but I'll be a heifer soon, God willing.

I was born and grew up under sub-standard circumstances and in oppressive conditions of servitude. Our housing was a poor barn where the roof leaked, and where there was no heat in winter and the toilet facilities were more like an open sewer. Like some place with landlords who didn't care. I didn't mind that so much, for it was all I had ever known, but the way our owners treated us was abominable. I mean, we were constrained, closed in much of the time, and my father was fenced off in another field and they didn't even let him decide that my mother was the one he wanted to be my mother. They just decided for him. They called it breeding. But, in so far as I was directly concerned, it must have been all right, for I am here, aren't I? Would I be here if my mother weren't my mother, or even if my father weren't my father? I myself am the product and culmination of the lengthy selection process that went on for decades or centuries before I came into being. So it must have had something good about it. But, for most of my older brothers and sisters, it wasn't good. Wasn't good at all.

Some of my uncles they took away and did horrible things to them when they were young, and then called them steers or oxen and hitched them up and made them pull plows and wagons for the rest of their lives. And added insult to injury by calling the wagons ox-carts. And even worse, my older brothers and sisters would just mysteriously disappear from time to time, usually a day or two before our masters had a big party. On those days you could smell the aroma of flesh cooking in the ovens and barbecue grills of the human folks. And as if that were not horrible enough, what our owners would then do is pull up their chairs and gather around a big table and slice up the cooked body of one of my brothers or sisters, and then eat him. EAT him. Or her. It was enough to turn one of your stomachs.

My mother they took away from me and wouldn't let me have any more milk. They gave me some horrible slop instead, mixed with some kind of stuff that was supposed to be good for you but tasted awful. I cried out and even tried to moo a little but it didn't do any good. They put my mother in another place and started pulling my milk out of her, but still didn't give any of it to me. They drank it themselves or made butter and cheese out of it that they could eat with the meat they were cooking.

You never know what's in store for you when you live your life in captivity like a slave in a little cabin, where you can never make decisions for yourself because someone else is always making them for you, because somebody else owns you and is always telling you what to do. Nobody likes to have others tell them what to do, but they DO like to tell OTHERS what to do. Well, animals don't like to be told what to do all the time either, even though we are owned by people who have the legal right to do what they want with us.

When I got old enough to start thinking, I started thinking. And I thought there must be a better life to look forward to, somewhere else than here. Maybe across the river there are places where an ox doesn't have to pull an ox-cart all the time and calves can run around without being owned by someone and without the threat of being sold far away from their loving families or, even worse, of being slaughtered and being sliced up for dinner, when some inhuman human owner out there, on a whim, happens to want to serve veal scaloppini at his next party.

So one night I decided to make a break for it.

There was no easy way to tell my parents goodbye, but that couldn't be helped. Sometimes you have to take matters into your own hooves, so to speak, and do what you have to do.

So I went away. I swam across the river to a new land. I was away for many weeks, and although there were people trying to catch me, I was wary and kept my freedom. Whether they would have bound me up and sent my back to my owners or kept me for themselves, I couldn't say. But I could go almost any place I wanted, and eat grass and stuff wherever I found it, as long as I did it mostly at night and stayed on the lookout for trouble in the daytime. Trouble of course meant people, even some of those people who lived across the river. I rather liked the life of a nomad, although I was hungry much of the time . . . Some nights I even wished I had a bucket of that slop my parents' owners used to give us. And then I thought about my parents too. The truth is that I missed them, and as the days went by I missed them more and more. And I learned something too. I heard about how one of us who was locked up somewhere in a big city up north found a solution to the problems of the oppressed bovine species, and got revenge for some of the injustices that had been heaped upon us during our decades and centuries of servitude. I decided to return home with a similar plan. An idea. I don't think my parents ever had an idea in their life, but now I had an idea and I would take it home with me and maybe try it out.

So I went back home to the farm where my parents were, and it was a joyous reunion, seeing Mom at the end of the barn, and Dad on the other side of the fence, although we could only rub noses through the wire.

"We are so glad to see you my dear," they said, in cow language. "In spite of having many of your sisters and brothers still around here, we have missed you the most. I wish there were some way we could properly celebrate your return."

And then I heard our owners saying to each other, "The calf looks thin. The calf has lost weight. We need to fatten up the calf."

Fatten the calf! I caught my breath. I had heard those words before. They only told me one thing. *Fat calf* meant prompt disappearance, followed by rich appetizing aromas wafting up from the kitchen chimney of the house where the human folks lived. But this time it didn't frighten me. I knew what I would do . . . I had an idea. And now, it seemed, was the time for it.

So I said to my parents, who wanted to celebrate, "That's okay, I have an idea for a party."

It was late fall then, and it got dark early, so the human people had to use lanterns in the barn for light at evening milking time. Sometimes they would leave a lantern on late, after the milking was done and they were all back in the master's house for the night.

I was pretty strong for my size, and when my chosen moment came I broke out of my stall and got my mother and the other six or eight cows and little ones to leave the barn.

When they were all out and everything was quiet, I went back in there and carefully kicked over the lantern and set the barn on fire. Now the good news is that the home of our owners was attached to the east end of the barn and the wind was blowing from the west (as I had planned in choosing my moment). And, as I had hoped and planned, the old wooden house caught on fire from the barn almost immediately, with our tyrannical owners all asleep inside, getting what they deserved.

They didn't have fire departments in that part of the county in those days, so the ashes smoldered on throughout the night and the next day until the fire finally burned out twenty-four hours later. But the aromas of roasted human flesh were delightful. My family and I were vindicated after generations of suffering at the hands of our domineering and oppressive masters.

The smell of meat still cooking slowly over the embers made your mouth water. For the next week my parents and relatives and I gave up our vegetarian diets and became meat eaters like you wouldn't believe. Now, meat is something you can chew on, better even than chewing on your cud. It was indeed a joyful occasion, a prodigal feast. Once again my grateful parents said to me, "Welcome Home."

THE END

A Few More Days

The best way to acquire wealth, without a doubt, is to inherit it, if you possibly can. The next best way is to use you brains, assuming you have some. The least appealing way is to slog along using your arms and legs and back muscles. But there is one other way that we will come to later on in this story.

I was born in the Old Country, in Eastern Europe, on a nice farm, or country estate, that my father had inherited from HIS father, my grandfather, who died two years before I was born.

When I was very young we had several servants in the house and many workers in the extensive fields around the place. We grew grapes that were sold to the local wine-maker, sunflowers that went for vegetable oil, and hay and corn that were sold around the county after we had fed our own farm animals. Sounds idyllic, doesn't it?

But by the time I was old enough to go to school I noticed that we didn't have as many servants as we used to have. Soon there were only two left, our cook, Hilda, and her husband, Philippe, who was sort of a general handyman. About that time we lost the section of land where the grapes were grown. I learned later that we had had to sell it, along with a lot of animals, to pay our debts. Gambling debts, they were. It seems that my father spent most of his free time gambling when he wasn't drinking.

I had an older brother and sister, Vladimir and Raquel. Vladimir was the muscle type I just spoke of, happy as a cow, working in the fields whenever he could. He even dropped out of high-school because he liked working the soil and because Father needed him more now that he had so few regular farm hands left. My sister was the brainy type; by that I mean she used her brain, and as soon as she was old enough - seventeen I think she was - she left home and struck out for the Big City. I was thirteen then. I had always been close to Raquel, and her departure came as a terrible blow to me, coming as it did less than a year after our mother died of tuberculosis, or consumption as it used to be called.

I remember it well, when Raquel left. She gave me a big kiss - a real kiss - the first time any woman had ever kissed me like that, and said that she would do something for me one day, but that she couldn't stand the miserable life we were being dragged down into, there on the farm. No more servants, no more fine new clothes, no money for parties or anything nice. She hated the place and I was beginning to hate it too. But I was stuck there.

After my sister's departure, I began to realize that a girl I knew at the next farm down the road - Angelique was her name - was rather pretty and seemed to like me, so we started seeing each other on a regular basis. That is, as regular as our farm chores and school schedules would permit. I was still in school, but I hated the rich kids there, whose fathers had gotten where they were by being on the right side when a new political group took control, or by having a relative in the tax office.

Considering the sad condition of his finances, my father got the bright idea of doubling our land holdings by having me marry this Angelique because her family's lands bordered ours. That was all right with me; I was sixteen by then and my hormones were ready to go, and I thought that maybe that way I could get out of the house and away from my father and Vladimir, neither of whom I ever liked much anyway.

So I married her and moved to her place, but it turned out that life was no better there than it had been before. Angelique was pretty and sweet, and very gentle, but rather sickly and frail, and when our son Karl was being born, she nearly died. After that she devoted most of her attention and strength to caring for the kid while I was expected to work in the field like a common farm hand.

That went on for the next three or four years, and that's the way things still were when I went to the Big City to visit my sister Raquel, whom I had not seen for a long time.

She had been in the city almost ten years by then, and shared a lavishly appointed seven-room apartment with another woman who was her partner in business. Their business was running a beauty parlor on a fashionable shopping street downtown. After some hugs and a couple of kisses she told me how things were with her, although it was obvious she was doing quite well. "The real money," she explained, "doesn't come from doing women's hair and fingernails. It comes from what you learn."

"What you learn? What do you mean by that?" I asked.

"These women talk about anything and everything. A lot of them have rich husbands who are in government or politics or big business, and let me tell you, there is a lot of dirt in this world besides what's under your plow back home. And believe me, it goes all the way to the top. A lot of them make money by what they know about other people, so why shouldn't I?"

I have to admit I was impressed, while at the same time feeling a little embarrassed by the old-fashioned cut of my clothes from the country

"You know," she continued, "you really should come live in the city, Henry. There are plenty of people here getting rich who are not half as smart as you. There are jobs where you can do very well, if you keep your politics straight and know some of the right people. I might be able to help you find a nice spot in the City Government."

"I have a wife and kid back home, Raquel. He is little and she is not very well."

"Leave them there. She has family; she will be okay."

"You may have a point . . . I do like your place here!" I said, as I looked around. "This is really nice."

"All it takes is money."

"I wish I could. I'll think about it anyway."

But I had my mind made up even before I got back home. Yes, I would make the move. But when I told Angelique, she insisted that she and Karl come too. I tried to convince her that I should go alone at first, and get established, and then they could come and join me. I did not relish the idea of having a wife and kid around my neck while I was trying to get a job and make my way in the Big City, but she insisted. Finally we compromised and decided that she would come but that the kid would stay with his grandmother.

By a fortunate coincidence, we made our decision the same week my father died. He fell off the tractor that he had never learned to drive properly, and hit his head and died immediately. That of course delayed our departure, as I had to stay for the probate of his will and the property settlement. Raquel was to get the little bit of cash and securities that Father still held; Vladimir and I were to share the farmland. The land, however, had been heavily mortgaged, to pay off gambling debts of course, and was worth only a few thousand more than the outstanding amount owed on the note. Vladimir, who somehow loved the land but knew I hated it, made a very modest offer to buy me out. I objected to his stinginess, but the city beckoned, and I wanted out of there, so I accepted his offer, and off I went to the Big City, with Angelique in tow. Anyway, the money from Vladimir would do for our expenses there for a few months or maybe a year or two while I went about finding a suitable position and getting established.

Now my life had suddenly changed, and I envisioned prospects of an exciting future to look forward to, knowing that I was going to have a good income and some of the finer things in life. We rented a furnished apartment with some expensive-looking period furniture that I hoped people would think was mine. Moved in, hired a cook and a butler, bought some stylish city clothes in spite of their outlandish expense, and prepared to take on the city's high society while I went on looking for a proper job, or "position," as I preferred to call it. It was lucky I had the money from Vladimir for the sale of my share of the farm, even if he did gyp me on the deal.

Several weeks went by, and I was enjoying the city while I went on looking, but I wasn't doing too well finding the right job. Raquel gave me some leads that looked interesting but went nowhere, and I was beginning to get worried as my funds were running down faster than

I had anticipated. I chafed at the sight of other young men with their fancy clothes and fancy women eating expensive dinners at fancy restaurants - men that were no smarter than I was, maybe not even as smart, but who just happened to be in the right place or knew someone with the right connections.

Then Raquel came through with something. The husband of a client of hers was leaving his assignment as Secretary of Deeds and Records at City Hall, and if I hurried I might be able to get the job. So, I hurried, and was accepted, but oh, was I disappointed! The salary was only one third of the minimum I figured I needed. I complained to Raquel. "Take the job, Henry," she said. "You will be in a position to know what is going on, and you will find it can be of great benefit to you."

"Benefit?"

"Yes, benefit. Financial benefit. The City Hall Records Office is an ideal spot to find out about people. And information is money. Especially information about people."

I hesitated. "You mean, blackmail?"

"That's your word, not mine. 'Opportunities,' I would say."

So I took the job. But the opportunities were slow in coming, or else I didn't recognize them, and I began to wonder whether Raquel had some talent that I did not inherit when the family genes were passed around. And even with my job, which didn't involve much work really, my financial resources continued to shrink. I decided to let the butler go, and began to berate Angelique for her little shopping sprees or for spending on anything beyond basic necessities. We cut out social entertaining almost completely, as I scoured the inner workings of my job for the collateral opportunities Raquel insisted were there. It seemed I was stuck again, getting nowhere. Meanwhile, Angelique's health continued to deteriorate, and without the psychological boost of being able to go on spending freely and lavishly in the Big City, she took to her quarters and thereafter spent much of the time in bed surrounded by her soft pillows.

One or two doctors we contacted could find nothing seriously wrong with her. Then a third diagnosed her as having a deep-seated tuberculosis that had probably been lying dormant for some years. Like my mother had had. The long-term outlook was not good.

I suggested sending her back to her mother on the farm, where, I pointed out, "the air might be better for her," but she would have none of it.

I am your wife," she insisted, "and my place is here by your side." Of course, by that time, considering her weakened condition, her phrase, "by your side" was more figurative than literal. But be that as it may, I did feel some obligation toward her. She had been my means for escaping from an intolerable situation at home years before, even though now she was becoming almost an intolerable situation herself. And I began to imagine how much faster and further I could have risen in city society and importance if I had been able to come here alone, without her, as I had wanted to do in the first place.

Angelique's condition continued to get worse, and that was the situation that existed when Raquel came by the apartment early one evening. "How is dear Angelique?" she asked, with a benign expression of concern and sympathy. We looked in through the partially open door to my wife's bedroom. She was asleep there, supine, with her wrists crossed over her breast, like a saint. We tiptoed back out into the hallway.

"There is something important I must tell you, Henry. But this is a terrible time to have to say it." Raquel's voice sounded slow and choked up, and she even wiped a tear from her eye on the sleeve of her silk blouse.

" Yes, what?"

"I hate to bring this up now, what with Angelique the way she is and all." Her voice was hesitant, and her eyes were moist with thoughts of her dear sister-in-law.

"Yes? Well, what is it? Go on . . ."

"It's just that the timing is so bad," she managed to say. Then her voice suddenly cleared and strengthened, and her eyes took on a penetrating clarity. "All right," she said, "I'll tell you. It's this: I have the answer for your finances."

"You mean you found me a better job?" I said as I drew her to me and put my arms around her.

"Not exactly. I have learned, through my sources, of a once-in-a-lifetime opportunity for you. A prominent and very wealthy man in the city has a lovely young daughter named Cherie who is expecting a baby."

"All right. That's nice. So what?"

"So nothing, except that she is not married."

"So, she gets married. She won't be the first woman to get married after the fact. What's the problem? Where's the guy?"

"The problem is that the 'guy,' as you call him, is already married and will take no responsibility for the deed."

"So, the father gives her some money and tells her to go to Switzerland for a couple of weeks. Or maybe nine months."

"No. The father is Old School and threatens to disown her."

"Well, so that's tough. What's all this leading up to, anyway?"

"The girl's aunt is a customer of mine. She is also rich, very rich, and has a better way in mind. She is willing to pay a large dowry - and I mean very large, in the millions - to a proper and decent young man who will pose as the father of Cherie's unborn child and take Cherie in marriage. It is very important for the social position of the whole family that there be no scandal. But because she is already three months along, they can't wait more than a few more days.

"It would be the end of all your money problems," Raquel continued. "From now on you could do whatever you want, go wherever you want, buy the house you want, entertain any way you want, be a personage people will know and respect in the city. Be somebody."

"What's in it for you?"

"Oh, don't worry about me. I will be all right." But I knew what her little smile meant.

"Come on, Raquel. I can't do that. Hey, I'm still married. To Angelique. You know that."

"She has no life ahead of her in any case. She is practically in a coma most of the time already."

"In any case? What are you thinking?"

"Well, the matter is urgent. I have described you to Cherie's aunt and she has agreed to the arrangement, but we have to act promptly - now - or she will find someone else. You can understand why promptness is important to her and to Cherie."

"But . . . but . . . Angelique . . . " I stammered.

"A soft pillow, with a little pressure over her face - that's all you need do. You'll probably be doing her a favor, in her state. Help her go to a happier world that awaits her up There," said Raquel, lifting up her eyes toward the Heavenly Kingdom. "And do yourself a favor. And poor little Cherie too. Everybody will benefit this way."

I took a deep breath. "Well, maybe you're right," I said, although at first I was somewhat bothered at the thought.

I took another deep breath, pushed the bedroom door the rest of the way open, and went on in. There she was, lying motionless on her back, her pale face aimed at the ceiling. Pale. "Deathly pale" were the words that came to my mind. In fact, I would have thought her dead already, but her eyes were now open. Wide open. Wider even than they had been when I kindly asked her to marry me, seven years before.

Wide open, in a fixed stare.

She turned her head slightly toward me. "It's all right, Henry," she said softly. "I'll be gone soon. Just give me a few more days."

She had heard everything.

THE END

Like I Said, an Ordinary Guy

Like I said, Jack Morrison was a fairly average guy. Oh, he had a few peculiarities and idiosyncrasies; I guess everybody has. And even ordinary people can surprise you. Sociologists and psychologists and people like that will tell you nobody is really average.

The thing I noticed about Jack was that there seemed to be a sort of hypocrisy about him. Not exactly hypocrisy, but a kind of artificiality, vaguely mysterious, that you couldn't quite put your finger on. It was as though you never knew what he was thinking. Of course, you never *really* know what *anybody* is thinking, but sometimes you may have some idea. With Jack you didn't even have that.

It was as though he were always enjoying some secret humor at someone else's expense. And he seemed to set different standards and expectations for himself than he expected of others, sometimes higher, sometimes lower, but different.

He was that way in high school, where the boys who talk the most or boast the most may be the ones with the fewest successes or, shall we say, conquests; and likewise, the girls who flirted the most in school and college were the ones who did the least. I mean, the ones who lost their virginity early on usually did so quietly, without talking about it. It was the boys who did the talking, and passed the gossip around. Marie was the other kind, lively and talkative, flirty and fun, but she hung on to her virginity all through high school and long after she graduated.

Jack, even back in high school, was always trying to lift himself above his innate ability level. He was really a natural C+/B- student, good enough but no genius, but he almost knocked himself out trying for a few B+'s and A's.

And he was always a natty dresser, well groomed, while most of us in those days were pretty sloppy in our attire and looked as though we didn't care anything about appearances because, in fact, we didn't. After college Jack got a job with an insurance company where he could always wear a coat and tie. He liked that, liked the appearance of success and prosperity. Anyway, he was already doing pretty well and making some money, something the twins never did. I'll tell you more about the twins in a minute or two.

I liked Jack well enough, although I never really understood him, never completely trusted him, I don't think. Don't know why. Maybe because his analytical approach to things was different from mine - grades, clothes, appearances, women - things like that. But in high school Jack and I went around in the same group that included Eric and Harry Johnson, who were the twins, and Betty Colinsky and Marie Colinsky, who were not twins and were not even related, or so they said. How two people named Colinsky could be unrelated is beyond me, but there it was. Anyway, they were very different from each other, whereas the Johnson twins were carbon copies. (I wonder whether anybody these days knows what a carbon copy is.)

In high school there was always a lot of joking about romance and sex and all that, and claims and counterclaims regarding exploits and conquests, among the boys anyway, although much of it was just hot air. Fornication in that generation didn't usually start in high school, as it apparently does now, and often not even in college. And, like I said, it was doubtless a true saying that those who talked the most did the least.

Marie and Betty were both attractive young women, and were what we used to call "popular" in school. "Dates" in those days just meant taking a girl out to a football game or the movies and a soda at the corner drug store or Hot Shoppe where we used to gather sometimes, especially Saturday nights.

Marie was the more outgoing and venturesome of the Colinsky girls, and while most people would say Betty was better looking, Marie had more dates and consequently was the subject of more whispered corridor talk, although I am sure that's all it was - just talk.

When the Johnson twins graduated from college they promptly married the two Colinsky girls. The two men had gone through ROTC together and graduated as Second Lieutenants in the Army Reserve. They had a double wedding and both Jack and I served as groomsmen. I was going steady then, with Julie, my college sweetheart that I later married. Jack was still unattached.

It was about that time that the United States, coupling the manifestation of its destiny with the obligations it had assumed as the world's policeman, launched another overseas invasion which required calling up the reserves, including the Johnson twins. Poor guys, they had only been married five months when they were shipped off to a distant land to fight, for and against, democracy and terrorism, respectively. They thought they were going overseas for one year, but their tours were unexpectedly extended to eighteen months.

In the interest of old times' sake, Julie and I would invite Jack and the two young Mrs. Johnsons over for dinner from time to time. We always enjoyed their company and of course were sympathetic to Betty and Marie in their loneliness, but it wasn't long before I realized Jack's feelings for Betty were more than altruistic sympathy. The truth is they were carrying on an affair and had been doing so ever since the twins went off to war, maybe even before that.

Jack seemed very happy with the arrangement. Satisfied might be the better word. Rather more self-satisfied with himself than satisfied with her, perhaps. There was a proud contentment, almost a quiet pompousness about him, although he never openly acknowledged the affair and certainly didn't advertise it or tout it about. But it was clear to me what was going on. I don't know whether Marie knew about it or not. She and Betty shared their sorrows on each other's shoulders for a few weeks after the men left for the war, but after that they didn't see much of each other except at our house.

Betty also looked happier now than she ever had with Eric, as her inner contentment began to show through. I even wondered whether she should have married Jack in the first place, although as far as I know he never asked her. And now of course I was picturing a theatrical triangle when the twins eventually came home.

But such concern was soon made academic by the sad and sudden news of the death of both twins, just one month before they were due to return to the USA. Well, at least now there would be no big confrontational scene.

After seventeen months abroad, they were killed in action, on different occasions, only two days apart. One was killed by the explosion of an improvised land mine that demolished his vehicle and killed all three occupants, and the other was killed two days later, shot through the head by friendly fire while returning unexpectedly early from a night reconnaissance foot patrol.

The two young widows were severely aggrieved naturally, and pretty much withdrew from the outside world and society in their sorrow.

It was then that my boss sent me on a South American assignment for six weeks to check on some of our company's operations down there.

A couple of days after I returned, I ran into Jack at the mall. "By the way," he said, "did I tell you I am getting married?"

"Well, congratulations," I said. "I am sure you and Betty will be very happy."

"Betty? Who said anything about Betty? Marie Colinsky is going to be my wife."

"Marie?" I stammered. "But I thought you and Betty . . . "

"You don't think I'd want to marry a woman who would cheat on her husband like Betty's been doing all this time, do you?"

I was . . . speechless.

Well, like I said, even ordinary people can surprise you.

THE END

Turkey in the Straw

Our golden retriever, Gwendolyn, is the sweetest, the gentlest, and most loving creature on four legs - or even two legs - that you ever saw. Like collies, golden retrievers are justly known for their tolerance and friendly nature, and make ideal pets and companions, especially in families with children and babies where the tolerance and good nature of most pets might be pushed to the limit.

Gwendolyn's life was people. Specifically, our family. In spite of her breeding as a bird-dog, Gwendolyn never showed any interest whatsoever in the feathered species, and not much interest in other dogs either, for that matter. It was people she loved, played with, lived with, wanted to be with.

So you can imagine my astonishment when, one Saturday afternoon, after wandering off from our country home for a couple of hours, Gwendolyn returned with her body all wiggly with smiles and excitement, her tail swishing about like an airplane propeller, and with a freshly killed seventeen-pound turkey in her mouth. Not a wild one, but a domesticated variety. I wouldn't have thought she could get her mouth around it, let along carry it. But here she was, as proud as a General of the Army Who Had Just Returned from Battle. She dropped the bird at my feet and sat, smiling at me, awaiting a pat on the head and a commendatory "Good Dog."

What to do? I couldn't breathe life back into the bird and make it flutter away. I didn't even know where it had come from. It certainly looked like a strong, healthy young bird, still warm, not something I would want to just throw away in the garbage, so I gathered up this mass of dead-weight meat and feathers and jammed it into the freezer. My wife would soon be back from her ladies' club meeting in the city; maybe she would know what to do. She is smarter than I am and always good in minor crises.

So I just sat down to read the Saturday paper which I hadn't seen all morning.

When my wife did come home and I told her what had happened, she went straight to the heart of the matter and said we had to find out who the turkey belonged to and make amends.

So we spent two days of discreet inquiries all over our corner of the county, talking in the abstract to gas stations, convenience stores, feed and grain operations - places like that - asking in general terms for information about who around here might be raising chickens and turkeys.

It was through the farmers' market that we identified a number of remote possibilities, but only one that was close enough to be even reasonably likely, a little farm just a mile away from our house, but on the other side of the woods, which made it about five miles by road. Volmer was their name. John Volmer. It seems they raised mostly chickens but also had a few turkeys, sort of as pets. But we still didn't know what to do, and after a couple more days of worrying and fretting, we still had not made a decision and could not agree on how to face the unattractive prospect of telling them. Maybe we could somehow work up to it slowly, I thought.

Then a strange thing happened, and we read a "Dear Abby" letter in the newspaper about an almost identical case of someone's dog stealing a neighbor's chicken and bringing it home. Abby's advice was to do something nice for the offended neighbors, like taking them out to dinner or something like that. But she had no explicit advice as to how, or whether, to confess and take responsibility for the dastardly deed.

"That's what we'll do," my wife said. "I'll send them a card telling them we are inviting a few friends in for dinner from around the neighborhood and would like to have them join us."

"Good idea," I replied. "Soften them up some and make them feel a little beholden to us before we drop the bomb about Gwendolyn in their chicken-coop . . . or turkey-coop, or whatever it is." So we did it - sent out a nice note asking them over for the following Sunday afternoon.

Mrs. Volmer promptly telephoned to accept and to trade a few "do-you-know-so-and-so's" with my wife.

"She really sounds very nice," said my wife. "Maybe we should have tried to make friends with them when we first came here, three years ago."

"Well," I said, "there's plenty of time. We can still do it." The next day Mr. Volmer called to thank us once more for the invitation and repeat their pleasure in accepting in it. I was the one who answered the phone this time.

"It sounds delightful," he said. "We are looking forward to meeting you. And we'd like to bring something, maybe a bottle of wine . . . What're we having?"

"Well, since it's this close to Thanksgiving, I thought we'd have . . . uh . . . turkey."

THE END

Epilogue

Two or three months later, after we had seen the Volmers a few times and sort of gotten to know them, I decided, with my wife's help, that we should bite the bullet and clear the remains of our guilty consciences. When I had a chance one day I said to John, "There's something I need to tell you."

But let me back up a minute. Even before that famous dinner party, my wife and I disagreed on what we ought to do about the bird and what we ought to say to the Volmers.

She wanted to tell them everything right away and I thought we should hold off and think about it, at least for a while. And I felt we might as well cook the turkey for our dinner as it was certainly perfectly good, but she thought that was gross and wanted to chuck it and go buy another turkey or, better still, a ham instead, to get the taste of turkey out of our mouths, as she put it. So we went round and round, getting more and more nervous and upset with ourselves and with each other.

She said it wouldn't be right to feed them their own turkey. "It would be almost cannibalistic."

"You want to waste that beautiful bird?" I insisted. "Probably specially bred for taste by people who know turkeys. The Volmers must be experts and might appreciate its fresh country flavor. They should know what's good."

And as for telling them about Gwendolyn's part in this, I felt that there wasn't anything to be gained by doing that. It wouldn't bring their pet back; and we could make all the amends we wanted and ease our consciences by contributing to the Red Cross or maybe the Audubon Society in their name, or perhaps making a donation to the garden club that Mrs. Volmer belonged to and loved. Anonymously, I thought, would be best.

Finally we compromised.

She agreed we would serve the turkey for dinner so as not to waste a good bird and because we might not have been able to find such a fine one at the market anyway.

And I agreed that in due course we would make our confession to the Volmer's, as long as we didn't have to do it right away. Work up to it slowly, was my idea. I would let out the grim facts of the case gradually, sympathizing at first, then confessing, and finally contritely apologizing. Of course, I wouldn't connect the loss of Volmer's turkey with the turkey we had eaten for dinner that Sunday. No need to go that far; that would be too much. Unnecessary and perhaps . . . upsetting. They could guess if they wanted to, but we didn't have to spell it out for them and throw it in their faces. And my wife began to accept that view too. I can't speak for Gwendolyn. She was definitely in the dog house. As you can imagine, neither of us was speaking to her.

So, as I was saying . . . When I saw John again sometime later, I took a deep breath and started in. It wasn't going to be easy. "There is something I need to tell you."

"Yes? What is that?"

" We were sorry to hear about your loss."

"Loss . . . ? What loss?"

"About your pet turkey. Someone said you lost one of your pet turkeys, and . . . "

He interrupted me to say, "Oh, you mean the one that fell in the well last year and drowned? Yes, that was a sad day for us."

"Well no," I said. "Didn't you lose another turkey a couple of months ago?"

"No," he replied, "the one that drowned in the well was the only one we ever lost."

John Harvard Fantoma

You may think that the guys up at Harvard are dull, privileged, rich students, or intellectuals and pinko tea-drinkers, and perhaps some are, but there are some pretty good games and practical jokes going on there too.

When I was a student, there was one chap we all knew who was rich but also great fun, named Phillip Finlay Mittleton. Mittleton with two "t's." Three "t's" actually.

Harvard by then was no longer a preserve just for rich kids; after all, I was there, wasn't I? But Phillip Finley, or Filfin as we used to call him, seemed to have more money than he knew what to do with. I mean, he was always looking for things to do with it. One day he rented the entire Hayes-Bickford's restaurant on the Square and had them give out free food and ice cream for twenty-four hours to anyone who came in. When we played Yale in football that year he hired an airplane to fly over Soldiers Field towing a banner saying BEAT BULLDOGS BLUE. Of course, blue and white were the Yale colors. Anyway, things like that.

By the middle of our freshman year, he was looking around for some really great, unforgettable, stunt. We had all heard of the time that four Harvard students barricaded Boylston Street with MEN WORKING signs at dawn one morning, and dug some big holes in the roadway with a jack hammer, then packed up and drove off in a cloud of laughter. Or the story about how during one Christmas vacation they took apart a classmate's antique Model T

Ford and hauled it up into his dormitory room where they reassembled it and had the engine running when he returned for classes in January.

Those were the stories that went around, and although I had my doubts as to the veracity of some of them, particularly the one about the Model T, it was just crazy enough to have been true.

Anyway, the tales of such unusual exploits excited the imagination of Filfin, and he had to think of something to top them all. Leave a legacy, he said. In those days, and maybe even now, Harvard was rather casual and loose about such things as class attendance, reporting in and out of the dormitories, or "Houses" as they were called, signing on and off campus. Those kinds of things. After all, you were supposed to be a man by the time you went to Harvard. A Harvard Man, of course. People generally minded their own business around Harvard, and the time-honored atmosphere of academic tolerance was definitely bolstered by a significant element of administrative indifference.

"I wonder," said Filfin one day, "whether any of the faculty or the staff in this place ever know who their students are, or even care, for that matter. Why I bet a ghost could go through Harvard and no one would be the wiser."

"A ghost?" one of us asked him. "What do you mean by that?"

Filfin hadn't really meant anything by it. But because he had been questioned he began to think and to try and make something out of nothing. So he drew himself up and retorted, "I mean, I'll bet a fictitious name of a non-existent student could go through Harvard and graduate just like anybody else."

It was never intended as a serious proposal, but it was an interesting wild idea that we all - there were six of us that hung around together - that we all seized upon. Could a mere name go through Harvard and graduate without a body attached to it?

"Listen, you guys," said Filfin, "I'll pay his tuition if you will divide up his classes among all of you. Sign him up for some easy course you have already had, or on a subject that you already know about, or one you are taking yourself. It won't be much work for anyone, just like auditing another course and turning up for an occasional exam. It'll be a lark that won't be forgotten at Harvard for the next three hundred years."

We thought it was an hilarious idea and wholeheartedly threw in our support, eagerly picking up on the proposed scheme, as we gathered around to choose his major, which was to be Government, and contemplate his program of study following in our own various footsteps. We gave him the name John H. Fantoma and bribed a clerk in the Admissions Office to move his name from "List of Applicants" to the list of "Entering Freshmen, Early Approval," and set about selecting the actual courses for JHF that each of us would cover starting in the fall term.

When we returned to the campus in September it worked out pretty much as we had planned. Fantoma had to take some basic courses in math and English and social studies his first year, but we always had a bemused participant in on the hoax to cover each course he needed. We went ahead and signed him up for courses that were the same as, or similar to, courses that we had taken or were taking. It wasn't much work, just fun.

I was a history major, so of course I got his history classes, which was fine with me. All I had to do was quietly make a classroom appearance for him at the beginning of the term, follow the posted reading assignments, and occasionally sit for a silly exam on stuff I already knew. It was fun signing John H. Fantoma and nobody was bothered or took any notice.

Fantoma went through his freshman year with a solid "gentleman's C" average amazingly easily. (In those days before "grade inflation" infected the system, sixty per cent of the grades given out at Harvard were "C's." The "B's" were hard to come by and "A's" were rare indeed, being only about 7% of all grades.) We simply had our man take easy courses for the most part from those we five had taken the previous year, usually using old papers and reports with a little editing so it wouldn't look too much as though Fantoma were copying.

We got Fantoma a post-office box address and had him sign up for the Glee Club and the Young Republicans Club and the Stamp Club, and pretty much left it at that. It would have been too embarrassing to put him up for any of the real clubs, like the SAE or the Porcellian. The Glee Club dropped him early on because he failed to meet the required minimum number of rehearsals, but, except for that, there seemed to be no impediment to his progress and no limit to what he could do. We celebrated the completion of Fantoma's first year with rum punch, much gusto, and many laughs among ourselves.

The next year, Fantoma's sophomore year, went much the same way. No problems, continuous chuckles up our sleeves, good fun. The only thing unusual that year came in the fall semester, when inadvertently two members of the cabal signed Fantoma up for courses meeting at the same hour. Afraid of bringing attention to the whole thing if we hastened too noticeably to change one of the courses, we just let him go on through the whole semester with the blatant conflict of classes. Fantoma hardly ever, or actually never, attended class anyway. It was perhaps the only time one person had ever taken two courses at Harvard at the same time, the same hour, on Tuesday and Thursday. Though unplanned, it was a New First, but it would not be the last.

Our fun went on for over two years, and it was now March of my own senior year and Fantoma was a second semester junior. Filfin had to line up some new blood to carry on the Fantoma Movement for the following year, when Fantoma would be a senior and the members of the original cabal would have graduated. He had no trouble in doing so, although my interest in the matter turned out to be, as they say, academic.

I hate to have to tell you this, but, with only two months to go before my graduation, something came up. During my final semester I had Fantoma in another history course, a relatively simple one called Post-Renaissance Comparative European Political History, a course I had never actually taken myself, so for a mid-term history paper Fantoma submitted a slightly modified version of a report I was writing at the same time for my course in The Influence of the English Royal Family in the Elizabethan Age. After all, Elizabethan England was also Post-Renaissance Europe, wasn't it?" It was a pretty good paper if I do say so, and I was quite proud of it.

Ironically, if it had not been so good, but more ordinary, perhaps it would not have attracted the attention that made for the trouble that soon followed. Anyway, on previous occasions Elizabethan Age material had satisfied the graduate assistants who were readers for the course in Post-Renaissance Comparative European Political History, and they were quite pleased with this latest submission.

But then something happened. It seems the readers for those very two courses knew each other and somehow got the two papers together and noted remarkable similarities beyond any probability of coincidence. Undoubtedly seeking their own personal advancement and renown within the system, they seized the day and took advantage of this whistle-blowing opportunity, excitedly bringing their discovery straight to the attention of Higher Authority.

Why the Authorities picked on me instead of on Fantoma is something I will never know, but somehow I was the one they decided to make an example of. An example to hold up to the entire student body and to the whole world.

The shock came in the form of a letter from the Provost's Office blandly stating that plagiarism at Harvard was "viewed with zero tolerance." (They couldn't have simply said will not be tolerated, or not allowed, or words like that. They had to say "viewed with zero tolerance." Yuck.) I didn't even know what the Provost's Office was, or what the Provost did, but soon found out. The Provost is some sort of chief executive, like chief executioner. So, because I had "obviously copied from the work of a respectable fellow student, John H. Fantoma," my matriculation was to be immediately terminated without expectation of reimbursement, and I was summarily dismissed, removed from the roles and records of registered Harvard students, and "asked" to vacate my residential premises at Eliot House and remove myself and my belongings from all Harvard grounds and properties, "with all due dispatch." They might as well have added, "From this time forth, for evermore."

The writer of this bombshell of a letter then had the effrontery to end with an exhortation that I should be ashamed for committing an abhorrent act which threatened to sully the positive name and sterling reputation of not only one of my (former) fellow schoolmates, John Harvard Fantoma, a "model of what a Harvard Man should be," but also Eliot House, my Class, the Harvard History Department, and "indeed," (their word), the entire complex of Harvard College and Harvard University.

THE END

Epilogue

I was quite taken aback and indeed depressed. But by then there was nothing left for me to do but go down to New Haven and finish my senior year at Yale, while Fantoma, facing fame and fortune, continued to fight fiercely at Fair Harvard. "Un-Fair Harvard" would have been more like it. Anyway, we had some good laughs along the way, and the last one was the best. Up to a point.

Later I learned from friends still at Cambridge that Fantoma graduated on schedule, attaining a grade average putting him in Category III, or second quarter of his class. Not bad. (They didn't have GPA's then.) He never showed up to receive his diploma at graduation; they had to send it to him at his post-office box. Filfin, who still lives in Boston, had photostat copies of it made and sent around to all of us who participated; I have it framed and hanging over my desk, as a memento. Maybe I am glad I myself never got a degree from Harvard. It is now quite clear they don't mean a thing anyway.

My Brother-In-Law Is a Jerk

My brother-in-law, Jimmy McIver, is a real jerk. I've never liked the guy much; he always seems to be putting on airs or trying to get something for nothing, and he's not even my brother-in-law actually. He is the husband of my wife's sister, whatever that makes him to me, but unfortunately he lives in our neighborhood, just down the street. So we get to see them from time to time, or rather, HAVE to see them, at family get-togethers, barbecues, etc. But I always feel that he is trying to put me down because he has a better job than I do, or because he has three kids and I only have one, or because he went to Harvard and I went to Slippery Rock. Things like that.

Anyway, getting on with the story: I was home one Saturday morning, reading the paper after a late breakfast, and vaguely pondering whether I had time to cut the lawn before the football game began, when the doorbell rang. Saturday doorbells usually mean Jehovah's Witnesses or Heart Fund drive I thought, as I went to the door. But no, it was neither. Rather it was just a young man, very clean-cut looking, perhaps in his late teens, wearing a wide smile and an open-collar shirt.

"Excuse me for bothering you, Sir," he said politely. "I am working my way through college and I have something you might be interested in."

Now, I don't usually welcome traveling salesmen, nor do I buy from wandering street vendors, but the young man seemed sincere, and I wasn't pressed for time, so I said, "Very well, let's see what you have."

With that he opened his briefcase and took out a somewhat oversize paperback book sealed in a clear plastic wrapping. The title read, "The Question Book - What Are Your Questions?" Underneath the title, printed in large letters that you could easily read through the plastic wrapping, were several enticing suggestions as to what might be discovered in the interior:

"WHAT ARE THE DOW JONES AVERAGES GOING TO DO?"

"WHO WILL WIN THE WIMBLEDON TENNIS NEXT YEAR?"

"HOW HIGH ARE GASOLINE PRICES GOING TO GO?"

"HOW CAN YOU MAKE LOVE LAST?"

"AND MANY MORE VALUABLE QUESTIONS"

"Let's open it up and have a look," I said.

"Oh, I'm sorry, Sir, I can't do that unless you buy it. Company regulations."

That should have been my clue, but the innocence of the shining face of that young fellow, and the natural interest I had in knowing what the Dow Jones and gas prices were going to do, overtook what should have been my better judgment, and I asked, "All right, how much is it?"

"Eighty-nine dollars, Sir," he said. "I have only a few left."

That should have been another clue; eighty-nine dollars is lot for a paperback, I thought. But the idea of predicting the Dow Jones had really piqued my curiosity, and that alone would have been worth more than any eighty-nine dollars. And furthermore I have to admit that some of the other come-ons cited on the cover did attract my interest. "Eighty-nine dollars?" I said. "That's a lot for a paperback."

"Oh," said the lad, "there are many other questions inside that I think you will find instructive." So I said, "okay," went and got my wallet; I just happened to have enough to give him the eighty-nine dollars. I took the book and peeled off the plastic wrap, as he and his smiling face turned and started to go.

Well, I could see right away that the book was a bunch of garbage. Things like:

What are the Dow Jones Averages going to do? ANSWER: They are going to go up and down.

And: Who will win the Wimbledon? ANSWER: A fine tennis player.

And: How high are gas prices going to go? ANSWER: As high as some people are willing to pay.

And - get this: How can you make love last? ANSWER: Do other things first.

I felt like poking him in the nose and accusing him of being what he was, a con artist, but that wouldn't have done any good. I'd been had. I tempered my tongue and corked up my fury, merely saying, "Hey, is this some kind of scam or something?" as he was heading off across the lawn.

"Oh, no Sir," he said as he looked back over his shoulder. "I'm sure you can learn a lot from that book."

I was already learning. Learning that I had been taken. Conned. But thinking fast and biting my lip, I said, "Wait a minute."

What I was thinking was that if my wife found out about this book of trash that I had paid eighty-nine dollars for, as she surely would, and the story got back to her sister's husband, that McIver son-of-a-bitch I was talking about, I would be a laughing-stock, and he would never let me live it down. So I calmly said to the young man, "I've got a suggestion for you. There's a fellow down the street, in the yellow house on the corner, named James McIver, who I know would just love to have a copy of your book. You should go see him."

"Oh, I've been there, Sir. He's the one who recommended I come see you."

THE END

The Moustache

I never was very successful with the fairer sex when I was young. I was, in fact, a rather shy guy, and by the time I was twenty I still had had no significant experience with women, hard as that may be to believe in this day and age.

After I graduated from college I promptly went to Spain for a couple of months, where something happened that gave me the idea for this story. The purpose of my trip was to practice speaking Spanish and thereby gain some of the authority I would need in the fall when I started teaching in my new job at a boys prep school back home, but that is really beside the point.

In those days, Spanish ladies were very proper, and the ones I was able to meet over there never did anything to narrow the great gap in my knowledge of women, the gap I would have so liked to close, but I did learn something, or thought I did.

There was one young woman - Valentina was her name - who attracted me inordinately. She was the youngest daughter in an aristocratic family and, although a few years older than I, she was still living at home under the watchful eye of her mother and of course was completely out of reach as far my basic urges were concerned. Nevertheless, Valentina and I worked out an arrangement whereby she would help me practice my Spanish on a regular daily basis, and soon she was comfortable talking with me about anything and everything. One day I must have commented on the many moustaches one sees in Spain. "Oh yes," said Valentina. "Women like moustaches. If a man kisses you who doesn't have a moustache, it is just like being kissed by another woman. *Es como un beso de otra mujer.*" Those were her words, and that's the truth. Wow. Ugh.

The image took me aback, but there it was, stamped indelibly on my inner eye, where it would remain for weeks and months to come. I never had the opportunity, nor the boldness for that matter, to try to disabuse her of her moustachio-philic philosophy, but I would never forget her admiration for the hirsute upper lip.

However, my immediate thought was, "Eureka! - This may be just what I have been looking for to open my way into the world of carnal happiness." So partly out of curiosity to see if what Valentina had said was true, and partly out of hope that it might bring on real results and a new romantic beginning in my life, I decided to do it. I would let the bigote begin. ("Bigote" is Spanish for "moustache.")

"Let the bigote begin" - it sounds like a new Brazilian dance tune.

By the time I got back to the States in September you could already see a shadowy horizontal smudge under my nose if you looked closely, and I had hopes that the shadow would soon darken and thicken and make me look like Errol Flynn or Clark Gable. I thought that perhaps in time I might be able to twirl the ends or at least twist them; I guess "twist" is the right word. Perhaps I would even be an Hercule Poirot, or an Adolph Menjou. My horizons expanded with my imagination.

Well, it took quite a while to get to the point of being able to twist anything, many months in fact, and by then I could rub it with the tip of my tongue or twitch my upper lip and feel the fuzz up against my nose. A pleasant sensation. Rather comforting. You know, like a security blanket. I even had some growth to spare and carefully trimmed the center portion, hoping to improve my looks as well as keep it out of the coffee. By then I could appreciate the practicality of the old moustache cups you used to see sometimes in antique shops and flea markets. I also cut and shaped the ends a little so they stuck out sideways.

Then I started making a conscious effort to begin dating more women now that I, like Samson, had developed this new hairy strength to back up my natural shyness. But the sad news is that most of the women I knew and tried dating didn't seem to like the moustache much, and some of them were even honest enough or rude enough to tell me so to my face. Then I met Maureen, the sister of a fellow I had known in college. Maureen was a lovely young woman I had always admired from afar, but I had never had the nerve to ask her for a date or anything, and until then she had never seemed to notice me. But now with the moustache I met her again, and with my growing confidence and new maturity and savoir faire I found it was easy and natural to ask her out, occasionally at first, and then fairly regularly. I knew she must like the moustache, although she never said anything about it. After all, she was dating me, wasn't she? That must have meant something.

By then the moustache had been growing for over two years, and had tails that were almost three inches long. And my affection for Maureen grew too, actually grew into love or at least a powerful lust for physical contact.

I was ready to get on with the process of learning more about women which had eluded me much too long already, and with my carefully trimmed and waxed moustache in hand, I decided the time had come.

So I had her over for dinner and a special evening with candles and soft music in the background. This was going to be the night. Things were going well, I thought, as we sat down to the table. "Swimmingly" was the word that came to mind. Then somehow the subject of the moustache came up, something we had never talked about before. Neither of us had ever felt any need to do so. I liked the moustache for the confidence it gave me, and Maureen must have liked it, and me with it, for here she was with me eating dinner by candlelight, wasn't she? So you can imagine my surprise when Maureen surmised my intentions - or at least my desires - and honestly responded, saying, "It's the moustache. I don't think I could ever really love anyone with a moustache like that."

I was almost dumbfounded. How could I have misjudged her so? Been so wrong? But, surprised though I was, I carefully responded, "Oh, Darling, I don't have to keep this stupid moustache. You should have told me before. It really means nothing to me at all," although, in truth, by then it had begun to mean a lot to me, representing, I thought, my strength and my masculinity and my virility. I had come to feel it was now very much a part of me, but clearly, in the interest of my career development as a youthful Romeo, it would have to go, and of course the reward would be well worth letting the thing go down the drain.

We changed the subject of conversation, got through the dinner in our usual friendly fashion with innocuous chitchat and a game or two of cribbage, and the evening managed to end itself just like so many previous evenings in my life had ended themselves. But, although I don't think she ever actually said it, she certainly left the clear impression that she might reward me with her treasured favors if only I got rid of the big M.

The next morning I couldn't wait to shave the thing off, and then as soon as the clock got to a respectable hour I called Maureen to make another date with her forthwith. This time I would take her to a fancy restaurant downtown, give her an expensive dinner, and ply her with wine and her favorite dessert. That and the new stiff upper lip ought to do the trick, if anything ever could. Finally I would make the breakthrough. Everything would be perfect. Was perfect. I had thought of everything.

When I picked her up she was more beautiful than ever, and I was more excited than ever, anticipating her response to the new me. Then a slight wrinkle appeared between her eyebrows as she looked at me and opened her pretty mouth.

"I take back what I said. I think I liked you better with the moustache."

I was speechless once again. The unspoken words lingered in my choked-up throat:

"Oh, that's okay, Sweetie. Let's have another date in a couple of years. I've waited this long; what's two more years?"

THE END

Money Money Money

I'm leaving here tomorrow. I've been here two years. Two years, two months, and one day, to be exact. I thought I'd stay at least five years, maybe ten, but I'm leaving tomorrow. That's what they said. That's what the guards told me two days ago. They didn't say why, just said I would be leaving, but that it would take three days to complete the paperwork. And then yesterday I got some more news that wasn't all good. Anyway, I certainly will be glad to be getting out of here. The horrors of spending time in a federal penitentiary are beyond anything you have ever read about in a detective story or murder mystery or seen in a one-and-a-half-star movie on crime and violence, but I'll say no more about that now, for I want to tell you the story of how I got in here in the first place.

I am not a criminal by birth, by nature, by upbringing, or even by the substandard socio-economic conditions of the neighborhood I grew up in. It was by choice that I became a criminal, or rather by choice that I participated in committing a criminal act. I have never considered myself a criminal, and now there is less reason to do so than ever. Anyway, you are only a criminal if you get caught. Even in high school I knew guys that were sometimes in trouble with the Law, but not me. I don't like trouble and usually I try to stay away from it every chance I get.

After high school I got a menial job at an auto-repair shop, which was all right with me. I had no great ambition and my needs were few until I got my girlfriend pregnant and married her and rented an apartment and the bills started coming in. And credit cards . . . the bane of our existence. My wife loved her credit cards and didn't seem to realize that the charges you put on a card are going to have to be paid off. Sometime. By somebody. By me. So I was in a pretty tight squeeze financially, with a wife who was really a very nice person but just happened to have high-class, expensive tastes . . . And then an opportunity fell into my lap.

One of my friends, named Akbar Bhutto, had been reading about how our CIA worked in foreign countries all over the world, typically influencing governments and politicians by the generous disbursement of money from a "black bag" of funds that they never had to account for, to Congress, or the GAO, or anybody else, or so it was said.

"Wouldn't it be interesting," he asked me one day, "if we could get our hands on some of that money? I think we could put it to better use than what the CIA is doing with it. It's not that we would be hurting anyone; it's money that doesn't really belong to anybody. The CIA doesn't have to account for it, and you could pay off your wife's credit card debt with your share and have a lot left over."

"Sure, but how?" I said. "Well, that will take some thought," Akbar replied. So he thought about it for several months and did a lot of research, and this is what he came up with. He had learned, or read somewhere, that the CIA was planning to put $50,000,000 into "reconstruction development" in Abdulistan, a war-torn region somewhere "over there."

"I didn't know the CIA was into reconstruction development," I told him.

"Of course they're not; that's just what they say. It's like a cover. It's like the 'humanitarian assistance' we administer through our military, which is a quiet way of getting our troops into places where we want them. And it works. And the CIA does the same sort of thing - been doing it for years, all over. Support for reconstruction lets the CIA get their people to the inside, where they want them to be, without having to go through a lot of political approval process or justify ulterior motives. It's also supposed to be good for the U.S. economy, as a lot of that money comes back by paying U.S. contractors working overseas."

Akbar continued his investigation and came up with the interesting news that this $50,000,000 was going to Abdulistan in cash. I don't know how he did it, but he even got details like dates and times and shipment schedules. He was convinced three or four of us could pull a heist, because CIA people were never personally attached to the money they threw around.

"But," I insisted, "even so, security around CIA must be tighter that a cow's ass in fly-time. You'll never even get in there."

"We're not going in there; we're getting it before it goes to the CIA."

"What do you mean?"

"We're going to the Bureau of Engraving and Printing, to pick it up on behalf of the CIA. That's where money starts - it's where they make it."

The details of his plan were precise and elaborate. They included bribery, architectural layouts, locks and security systems, schedules and names of guards and supervisors, the whole bit. The actual job came off surprisingly easily.

With two other collaborators we posed as CIA agents sent to pick up the 50 million. And believe me, it was a truck-full. There were forty bags that must have weighed fifty pounds each. They were probably hundred-dollar bills, but we signed the papers without checking on the contents, because, you might say, we have a trusting nature. Akbar even had employees of the Bureau of Engraving and Printing helping us load up. And off we went, to West Virginia where Akbar had a rental storage unit ready and waiting to receive the booty.

It was a perfect crime. Nobody hurt, nobody suffering from financial loss, nothing to link us to the theft. Or so we thought. We agreed that we would not touch the money, or even look at it, for a few months. It would be too tempting to dig our hands into it if we started opening the money sacks. We would go back to our regular jobs and act in a very normal fashion to ensure that we never were suspected of any wrongdoing. Too many otherwise successful thefts are exposed when the perpetrators give themselves away by a sudden change in their spending habits and lifestyles. After the first wave of concern and excitement among officials of the Establishment had worn off a bit, we would go back, pick up the loot, and plan the brilliant new lives that lay ahead of us.

But unfortunately, soon after the theft one of the guards that Akbar had bribed got into trouble with the law on an unrelated matter, a case of domestic abuse. He was accused of stabbing his mother-in-law in a family argument, but didn't quite kill her. Seeking to cut a deal by gaining favor with the prosecuting attorney, he squealed on us, telling them who we were and where to find us. I don't know how Akbar had ever let that out; no one was supposed to know who we were.

So the four of us got arrested and convicted of grand larceny and were sentenced to ten years in federal prison, with no possibility of parole until after a minimum of five years.

But there was one ray of light that still shone upon us. None of us had ever revealed the location of the storage unit where the cash was hidden. I'll be a good little boy for five years, I thought, get out and I'll have a rich future in store for me. Go back and get my share of the money and maybe go on to Mexico or the French Riviera and live like a king. For that, five years, or even ten, could be well worth it. Who said crime doesn't pay?

Well, if you have to know, I say so. You won't believe what happened.

A young lawyer from the Public Defender's Office, that I had never seen before, came to the prison to talk to me yesterday, and he explained why I would be getting out so unexpectedly. He was fresh out of law school, but had gotten interested in our case perhaps because he had a grudge with the CIA himself. Anyway, his investigations led to the reclassification of our crime of grand larceny. And this guy wasn't even on Akbar's payroll. He was just inquisitive and I think he wanted his name in the papers. Anyway, he was an eager little beaver, and for his own satisfaction in overcoming what he saw as a challenge, he got our grand larceny conviction reclassified as petty larceny, as normally applies in cases involving stolen goods worth less than $1,000.

What we had stolen was worthless paper. Damn, damn. Damn it all.

It seems the $50,000,000 we thought we had stolen was not, in fact, US dollars, but the equivalent of $50,000,000 in Abdulistan currency.

So that came as quite a shock. Not American currency? I have WASTED all this time in the pen? All for nothing?

But worthless paper? Yes, of course. Counterfeit. What would a ton of real Abdulistan money be doing in the United States? It was now quite clear what had happened. The Bureau of Engraving and Printing had printed it all up right here, stacks of counterfeit Abdulistan currency.

The United States is not always in favor of restoring or strengthening the economies of all the little countries around the world; not all of them are always on our side. On various occasions over the years the CIA has engaged the Bureau of Engraving and Printing to make great quantities of high-quality foreign currency that they then dump in certain countries to help destroy the economy of regimes that we consider to be unfriendly or a security threat to the United States. Our plans in Abdulistan were aimed at DEstruction, not REconstruction.

This is the same thing the North did to the South in 1863, right here in the USA. Most of the Confederate money ever made was counterfeit bills that were dumped with devastating effect on the Southern economy. In fact, the best quality Confederate money found anywhere came straight from the Bureau of Engraving and Printing in Washington. So they are good at it.

Fortunately, our theft had been pulled off without firearms or violence, which carry much more severe penalties; it involved worthless paper, and if that news had gotten out right away we never would have been convicted of grand larceny and given such prison terms, although of course none of us knew it at the time. There was really no strong case against us; no grounds for serious charges beyond pilfering and impersonating CIA government employees. So, that's about the end of the story.

The Bureau of Engraving and Printing was easily able to print up another batch of fake currency.

The young lawyer in the Public Defender's Office is getting national publicity and fame.

We have unjustly served two years in prison; and now I am getting out.

But I have wasted two years, my wife has taken up with another man and moved to California, and here I am wondering whether my old job at the auto-repair shop will still be open when I leave here tomorrow. So, I'm no criminal, and as far as crime is concerned, I say, Phooey.

Or . . . perhaps I should go over to Abdulistan and have a look, and maybe spend some money, mostly fake Abdulistan currency, that is. Especially if the Abdulistanis don't know the difference. I mean, if the CIA can do it, why can't I? And besides, that way I might even be furthering our cause and helping my own country, the good old USA . . . Somehow.

THE END

The World of Art

My name is Art Robinson. Of course it's Arthur really, but they call me Art. The interesting thing is that I have always liked art. Art with a small "a." When I was very young I thought that perhaps my name held the seeds of my destiny. You sometimes hear of cases in which a person's name suggests a connection with his profession or avocation, like Dr. Carver the surgeon and Archibald Ryder the famous polo player. However, it didn't work out quite like that for me, I mean art as a career and Art my name. But I do have an interesting story I would like to tell you about art. It may be that art is mostly in the eye of the beholder, but the story is true.

It all started at an art exhibit and reception at our local junior high school about seven or eight years ago. (Now they call it "Middle School.") It was one of those affairs where the public is invited but where 95% of those who come are parents or friends of the kids putting on the show, whatever it is. Like supporting the troops. It didn't make much difference whether the art work they did was good or not; they were your kids or your neighbors' kids and you had to support them in any case. Some of them were the younger brothers and sisters of my own students - I'm a history teacher at the adjacent high school where I have been for 29 years. So I just dropped in on the art show as sort of a civic duty, you might say.

The prettiest picture there was not a painting at all, but simply the face of the young art teacher managing the event. Wendy Harris was her name. She was fairly new at the school, and although I knew some of the other teachers, I had never met her before. She spoke graciously to the parents and others coming in and out, telling of her love of her work and her hopes and efforts to bring out the creativity of even a few of the kids. I had the feeling that it must have been a frustrating job and that many of those children just looked upon art class as a free hour, almost like recess. (Even teaching high school history had enough of its frustrating moments.) But on leaving I was struck by two landscape paintings I saw hanging in the hallway. I stopped a moment to look more closely and admire them, and noticed the artist's initials in the lower corner, WH. Of course - Wendy Harris. The paintings were good. Very good.

In college I had studied some art; also music. I would have liked to become an artist or a musician but was smart enough to realize early on that I did not have the requisite talent for either of those things, so I contented myself with singing in the shower and taking some courses in music appreciation and art history on the side. But I did learn a little something about art and kept up my interest in art even when I went into teaching history. I always felt that the art courses I had had in college enriched my life for years to come.

Art galleries and museums became sort of an avocation for me whenever I had a break or a vacation from history teaching. I learned to recognize and appreciate the work of the famous masters of various periods, and met several promising artists who are actively painting today. I occasionally bought one of their paintings that I knew was good if it didn't cost too much. I don't have much money - just my meager high-school teacher salary. (Magic Johnson, the star basketball player, makes 300 (THREE HUNDRED) times as much as I do.) But the exciting life is the life of the mind, and my physical wants are few, or so I try to tell myself.

Anyway, I think I developed the ability to distinguish between the good and the fair, and between the very good and the good, but I was always frustrated by the knowledge that, although I could recognize and admire the very good, I could never create it. The meager dabblings in paint that I surreptitiously attempted in the seclusion of my own home were so pathetic that I had to destroy them, swearing I would never admit to anyone how I had tried and failed. So it was back to the history books, where I was comfortable without having to be creative. The life and love that pervades art was beyond my reach, and I could grasp it only through appreciation of the works of others.

So, when I saw those two paintings signed "WH" in the hallway that day, I knew they were something special. I then made a point of getting to know this Wendy Harris, and even had lunch with her now and then. I felt I had to talk to her about her art. She showed me some more of her paintings, and they were exceptional, almost every one, although she didn't seem to know how good they were. She had never sold anything but had been giving them away to her students and her students' parents - people like that. Even to two of the janitors. I told her I wanted to buy one, and that she should charge. Charge a lot. I tried to give her some suggestions and told her all I knew about art, and what makes for good art, that I had learned when I was at Yale.

She was quite a bit younger than I, not much older than my granddaughter would have been, had I a granddaughter. I'm not a Picasso, so I really didn't have any delusions about our relationship developing into anything "significant," as they say, although it certainly was significant in its own way, for me at least.

I fell in love with her on a spiritual level, or cultural level, some special level that is known only to artists and art-lovers (and perhaps music lovers) when they connect in joint appreciation of the radiant and uplifting atmosphere of the art world. Perhaps only those who have experienced this emotional feeling and bond will even know what I am talking about. But Wendy did not realize she had the talent that I appreciated and envied but lacked myself. And, if the truth be known, I don't think she felt much of the emotional connection between us that I had been imagining.

I knew she had much more to give the world than just the hours she was putting in, teaching Middle School Art to hundreds of little knuckleheads who only really wanted a baby-sitter or a dodge-ball coach, and when I saw her occasionally I would tell her so. That went on for almost two years before she told me one day she was going to take my advice and go to New York to try her hand in the real art world. I thought she was doing the right thing, and, as I was still interested in this young person's potential career as an artist, I offered to give her a couple hundred dollars to help her along there at first until she could get a side job as a waitress or something. In my mind I had the stereotype of the typical aspiring musician or actress or artist in New York City sustaining herself by waiting on tables at the corner bistro. I think I saw in her a chance to vicariously enjoy a life I would have liked for myself had I still possessed the youthfulness that by then had slipped away, and the talent that I had dreamed of but never possessed.

So I wished her *bon voyage* and also gave her the names of some people I knew who were connected with the Art Students League and the American Watercolor Society.

New York must have swallowed her up, I thought. I heard from her once or twice in the first few months, telling me how big the city was, how noisy it was, that sort of thing. Not much about her art work. Then I didn't hear from her for quite a while. I think the last I heard was a Christmas card she sent to me at the school saying she was very busy, and that was over three years ago.

Then just last week I got a phone call from New York, from Wendy. What a surprise it was. A pleasant surprise. She was calling to apologize for not having written for so long and to tell me that things were going well for her. "I have made some pretty big sales and have quite a few important commissions lined up."

"I am delighted to hear it," I said.

Then she went on . . . "What I was really calling for was to make sure you are still there and have the same address."

"Yes, I'm still here," I replied, "here in my same little old rut."

"Well, maybe you should get out and go somewhere yourself."

"Oh, I'm all right here," I said, although in truth I did dream of a life in retirement where I could afford to drift from one great art museum to another, around the world - the Louvre, the Prado, the Uffizi, the Kroller-

Mueller, the Hermitage, the Tate, the Getty. (I had a list of fifty or more in my mind, most of which I had never seen even once.) But of course I would never be able to afford anything like that on the half-pay pension from teaching I would get when I finally did retire, especially considering that I still had alimony payments to meet from my only partially successful first marriage - actually my only marriage - many years ago.

But talking to Wendy and hearing about her progress in New York warmed my hibernating imagination as I conjured up the old dream and tried to visualize what success in the real art world would have been like. She repeated my address, saying she wanted to be sure she had it right because she wanted to write to me. "That would be nice; my address is still the same, except that four more digits have been added to the ZIP code, although they are not really necessary."

Three days later her letter came. "Thanks for helping me get to New York and the new life and the remarkable success that I have found. It wouldn't have been possible without you, and I am embarrassed for having neglected you for so long. Now it's my turn and I would like to do a little something for you from time to time, to show my appreciation. Thanks."

There was also something else inside the envelope. A check. I pulled it out. The amount of the check was $10,000. Wow!

Then I noticed that in the left hand corner of the check there were written the words, "for February." Wow-ee!

Like I told you, I knew her paintings were good. Very good.

THE END

The Beard

I had been going with Marie for almost three years. Had been. But that was over now. I was sorry to see it end; I had been very happy those years with her. She was the one who broke it off, not me. At least that's my story, although she will tell you something different. Women get funny ideas sometimes. It's not worth the effort to try and figure them out, and it's usually impossible anyway. Marie will say the breakup was my fault. Women will always put the monkey on your back if they can.

Anyway, things had been going just fine between me and her, and then out of a clear blue sky she started acting funny and accusing me of seeing other women on the side and having clandestine affairs and all that, which was absolutely untrue.

It dawned on me later that this could have been her way of covering up the miserable fact that she had found another man she thought she liked better than me, or who was richer than I was, or maybe just younger or something, but I did not pursue my inquiry into the matter. What good would it have done to analyze the cause of my misery only to prove that my hurt feelings were justified? We just ended it; it was as simple as that.

Have you ever noticed that when you can't have something it makes you want it more than you would want it if you COULD have it? Well, that's the way it was with me and Marie. Now that I COULDN'T have her I wanted her more than ever, but when I DID have her,

I didn't always want her that much. Some philosopher once said it is better to want something you don't have than to have something you don't want. I'm not so sure about that, but I have to wonder whether there's anything Marie wants that she doesn't have, now that she's gotten rid of me.

At first I directed my new-found free time to my studies and research in anthropology, and to the next book I hoped to publish. Try some new and different things. Get my mind off women. Maybe it would do me good to get a fresh look at life. A new perspective, or so I told myself. Maybe I had been in a rut or had been taking Marie for granted.

Then about that time something happened that affected my immediate future more than you would have imagined: I cut myself on the corner of my chin shaving one morning. A tiny nick really, but the next time I went to shave I left the chin alone and just shaved my lip and the sides of my cheeks. Then, after a few days of not shaving my chin, I could feel the beard beginning to sprout. "I wonder what it would look like if I let it grow," I thought. Well, after another week or two it got past the bristly stage and I was able to start stroking it and playing with it. Actually it was a rather pleasant sensation; it made me feel thoughtful and reminded me of Rodin's famous statue of *Le Penseur*, "The Thinker."

So I decided to let it go on growing for a while. But nobody liked it. My neighbors didn't like it; my friends at work didn't like it; I had to explain over and over again that I was letting let it grow because I had cut myself on the chin. But that story lost credibility with the passage of time, like after a couple of days. And the women I knew, and a few I didn't know, all hated it, and some of them even told me so to my face. Well, who needs women anyway.

Then an idea hit me. The beard could be a symbol of my new-found celibacy. A symbol of the mysteries of nature and my bad luck with women. And if the beard would help keep women away from me, so much the better. Because to tell the truth Marie was still on my mind, and I wasn't interested in getting involved with anyone else. I was getting a lot of work done, and I thought that perhaps the celibate life was best after all. And I figured that, in time, I would forget her completely.

So then I made a vow to let it grow and never shave it off as long as I maintained my life of immaculate morality. It would be a badge of my purity and determination, and proof that I could get along perfectly well without women dominating my life and telling me what to do all the time. I would keep the beard as long as I was celibate and I would be celibate as long as I had the beard. This I swore to myself in solemn oath. But I still went on thinking about Marie a lot, even though I kept telling myself I should just forget her.

And that's the way things were for several months and that's where this story should end.

But it goes on a bit longer, because after a while I found myself looking around at other women, and I began to realize that I was not cut out to be a hermit or a monk forever. In fact I wasn't used to being celibate for more than a few days at a time, and my body definitely was in favor of my meeting up with someone new. But I didn't quite have the old verve, the daring élan of days gone by, and of course, with the beard, no one liked me well enough to start anything.

This new and unfamiliar indifference of women toward me and my beard began to fuel my urges. The sweetness of the unavailable or the forbidden. I began to think of the joys of conjugal living - someone to talk to when you wanted to talk, someone you could take care of when you were feeling philanthropic, someone to go with you when you had two tickets to the opera, someone to sit on the other end of the see-saw, someone to help change the light bulbs and tell you when the TV was too loud, and someone to help make the bed in the morning. How had I been able to live alone without even an overnight visitor for almost six months? How could I go on this way? After all, I am a human being even if I am a curmudgeon.

So, I started going out again, trying to see some different women from time to time, but the bane of the beard continued to haunt me, and it turned all of them off. "Well," I thought, "maybe I have learned something. Maybe what I want is someone who can accept me as I am and love me in spite of the beard, for myself and for my inner being, and not just for my good looks."

But nothing much happened, and that went on for weeks, months even, as the beard continued to grow. I tried improving its appearance a little and trimmed it to look like Colonel Sanders, then General Ulysses S. Grant, then President Abraham Lincoln and other bearded icons who had gotten famous or had a reputation of having made out big with the ladies. No dice. Still, no one liked it, and I was convinced that no one liked me. So I swore again that I would keep it as a mark of my celibacy, and if

I ever shaved it off it would only be after I had once again proved my manhood.

I'm not very good at self-analysis, and I probably didn't really know what I wanted. I was enjoying my freedom from commitment: I could go anywhere, do anything, anytime, without having to give any explanations or excuses, even though, in my case, I wasn't doing anything that had any need to be explained or excused anyway. But the lack of a woman continued to be a void in my life which the beard, quite frankly, had not been able to fill, fulfill, or refill.

That went on for another year, and then one day at the mall I ran into Marie's sister Betty. At her suggestion we had a cup of coffee at one of those snack counters you always see at the intersection of two or three giant corridors.

"Where have you been? What have you been doing?" she asked.

"Nothing. Same as always. Hanging out. Working some."

"Why don't you ever see Marie anymore?"

"She doesn't want to see me. She's the one who broke it off."

"Well, I wouldn't know about that, but I feel you two should have another chance, and I think Marie might like to see you again, whether she would admit or not. Dick and I are having some people in for supper Friday - why don't you join us?"

Well, why not, I thought. See Marie, out of curiosity. See what was happening to her. How could that hurt? So I went to Betty's supper party.

She was there, looking good in a new low-cut dress and dancing shoes. Not beautiful perhaps, but, well, attractive. She always attracted me, and I could feel the old pull and tug once again that I had so often felt in past years.

"Oh, look at you," she said. "There's something new and dashing about you that I hadn't noticed before . . . Oh it's the beard! I love it! It does wonders for you," she said. Words like that. The rest of the conversation that passed between us was merely polite and perfunctory, considering the other guests present, but I got a definite impression that she would like to go back to where we had been, and start dating again.

It turned out that my impression was accurate, because the next day she called me up and invited me in, so to speak. Asked me over. All right. Why not.

So I went over and rang her bell. And there she was. I looked at her with renewed lust. Oh yes, she was enticing! As enticing as ever. I had never gotten over losing her, and now she was back in sight again. There, in front of me, in all her feminine glory, inviting me to - well - inviting me in, she said.

Just the words I had been yearning to hear. I licked my whiskers. But then I hesitated a moment before I answered her.

"Would you like to come in?" she repeated.

"Come in? What do you mean?" I muttered.

"Come in and stay for a while."

The powerful image in my mind was overwhelming. I grasped at my chin and stroked my beard for the security that I had now come to rely upon. I twisted my neck a little so I could rub it against my shoulder. A pleasant sensation. Comforting. Still she stood there, looking at me, expectantly.

"But I like my beard, I have gotten accustomed to it and I am really rather fond of it."

"What are you babbling about?"

"It's just a promise I made myself." I said. "I'm afraid it has become a part of me; I'm not sure I could shave it off. But I appreciate . . . "

"What on earth are you saying? Shave your beard? Why would you want to do that? I love your beard. It makes you look like somebody important. Like Abraham Lincoln. Or Colonel Sanders."

"Well, that's the trouble. I like it too. I have gotten used to it. It's a part of me now."

"Are you coming in or not?"

"Let me think about it."

"You men! I just don't understand you."

THE END

Bastille Day – Proving a Point

When I think back on my youthful years and how venturesome and ignorant I was, I have to laugh.

I was born in Algeria, North Africa, in 1942, in a little village called Mascara perched on the hillside above of the city of Oran. And that's where I grew up. It was beautiful country - wine country - with gentle slopes sprinkled with farms and vineyards spread along that strip of rich land between the mountains to the south and the Mediterranean Sea a few dozen kilometers to the north.

My ancestors had come from France, from the wine country of Alsace-Lorraine, and settled here, back around the middle of the nineteenth century. The story I heard was that the French government in those days was giving away land to Frenchmen who were willing to live here and thereby help the French expand their African empire. So then, for a hundred years, my family had been here in the business of growing grapes and making wine. Although at home we spoke mostly French, and my father had fought in the French army in WWII, I and the other family members of my generation definitely considered ourselves Algerian.

Even when I was young I worked in the fields - the vineyards - alongside Berber and Arab workers. Berbers, for the most part, were better farmers than the Arabs, but the Arabs talked more. My schooling was irregular, especially in the fall when the grapes had to be picked on exactly the right days. The grapes were more important than school. Even though picking grapes is hard work, I didn't care much for school either, so the grapes were all right with me. By the time I was fourteen and had more or less finished my primary education, my father died and I was working full time on the farm.

It was my bicycle that saved me from a boring life of drudgery and isolation, for with it I could cover the thirty or so kilometers to Oran in an hour. The city was exciting, especially after I met the daughter of a small restaurant owner who had been buying wine from our village since the end of the war. Bicycling back home at night took longer, almost two hours, as it was mostly uphill and it was late and I was always tired after my evening with Marie. Of course, to spend the night with her would have been out of the question. She was a very amiable girl, part French and part Arab and part I don't know what - Berber or Italian maybe. But not too religious, fortunately. Algerians have a lot of mixed backgrounds, but most of her friends and the customers at the restaurant were Arab.

I would usually visit Marie at the restaurant once a week on Saturday nights, and that went on for two or three years. So I got to know several of her friends and customers pretty well. They called me "Frenchy" because they said I speak Arabic with a French accent.

The restaurant was where I first began to hear about politics, and about how oppressive the French had been to the Algerians over the years, something I hadn't learned in school. I remember in school we had to learn about Napoleon and the Russians, and about the wars of the French against the English and later against the Prussians and the Germans. However, all that seemed quite far away from my village and far away from Algeria. But I liked reading about how beautiful Paris was, with its big avenues and places like the Louvre, and the Eiffel Tower, and the Bastille - places we read about in our history books.

Anyway it was at the restaurant that I began to hear more about politics, even though I never really understood that stuff. My friends there - the ones who were calling me "Frenchy" - talked about how "the day will come" and about how proud they were to be Algerian and not French.

"I'm Algerian too," I insisted.

"You don't sound like it," they would say. And although they didn't have much education either, they would discuss Algeria's right to autonomy or independence - things like that - things that didn't mean anything to me and my life on the farm and my bicycle and my Marie. But I liked my friends there, Arabs included, even though they did talk a lot.

Well, about that time the subject came up about a wonderful thing they called a movement. At first it sounded like a bunch of hooey to me. Its name was FLN which meant Front Liberation National. They insisted that anyone who did not support the FLN was not a true Algerian and started calling me Frenchy again.

"I'm not a Frenchy - I am Algerian," I again insisted.

"Well, why don't you prove it?"

"Prove it . . . ? What do you mean?"

"Go do something for the Front."

So, they decided that to prove my heart was Algerian I should go toss a bomb somewhere, calling the world's attention to the fact that the French had been abusing

Algeria, that Algeria deserved to be independent, and proving that I myself was an Algeria-loving Algerian. The target would have to be an outstanding monument or landmark. We wanted to get ourselves into the newspapers. We wanted to be heard. We had gotten nowhere by writing to the UN, to Amnesty International, the International Red Cross, the International Court of Justice, or any of those people. Now was the time for action.

So, there it was. The challenge. I was getting in deep and I began to have second thoughts about the whole thing. I didn't really want to cause a lot of damage or hurt people, but I couldn't be called a coward or an unpatriotic Algerian, could I? And besides, if someone was going to do it, the damage would be the same whether it was me or somebody else. But mainly I was frustrated by their picking on me and calling me Frenchy.

So I said, "All right, I'll do it."

But since nobody in the rest of the world notices us here in Algeria, and the Algerian people were already tired of bombs that had been going off occasionally around Oran for years, they decided I should go set off a bomb somewhere that it would be noticed, like in Paris.

I was seventeen by then but didn't like thinking too much about the fact that I might have to destroy something or maybe even kill somebody. I guess I am sort of a pacifist by nature, although I had never heard the term in those days, but I didn't like the idea of being considered a coward on top of that. I had to rise to the challenge and prove my mettle. At seventeen years of age I just had to.

Besides, I was thinking that it might be fun to visit Paris, the city that I had read about and heard so much about. Also, I had always wanted to see something of the world. At that time the farthest I had ever been was to Algiers, and I had only been there twice. Algiers is the largest city in Algeria, but although it is the capital it isn't much bigger than Oran. Anyway, I had already said yes, and had promised to do it.

So my so-called friends rigged up a home-made bomb and explained to me how to use it. Meanwhile I got out my old schoolbooks and started looking up things about Paris. The places that stuck out and had the most pictures were the Louvre, Les Invalides, the Eiffel Tower, the Pont Neuf, the Opéra, the Champs Elysées, the Bastille, the Cathedral of Notre Dame, and the River Seine. Places like that. My friends didn't know any more about Paris than I did, but we had to pick a target that would get us recognition.

I began to eliminate some of these places as targets. I eliminated L'Opéra because it said that's where there is music and I like music. I eliminated Les Invalides because it didn't seem right to risk hurting sick people who hadn't done anything wrong. And Notre Dame because I believe in God and didn't want to face his retribution in case he was one of those who didn't understand the justice of our cause. And the Champs Elysées and the Seine because although they were famous I don't know how you can blow up a field or a river.

That left us with a short list of the Louvre, the Eiffel Tower, and the Bastille.

Now there were pictures of all three of these in my old schoolbooks, which I showed to my cronies as we made our plans, or their plans for me, I should say. The interesting thing is that while there were both old pictures and new pictures of the Louvre and the Eiffel Tower, all the pictures of the Bastille were old pictures. And they were not even photographs, only old paintings and engravings. I knew it was a government building and had read that it was used as a prison before Napoleon's revolution. But the fact that there were no photographs of it in any of the books made me realize that the French government must be using it for secret operations and had made it illegal to take pictures there. The Secret Police and Special Agents were probably inside the building, plotting covert schemes, maybe even using it as a place for planning more repressive measures against us Algerians.

My geography book also had a map of Paris showing "Metropolitain" routes, which someone explained to me were trains that ran all over Paris, mostly underground. Wow! I'll have to see that! And there on the map you could see the Eiffel Tower, the Louvre, and the Bastille, marked as plain as day. It showed that the trains even stopped right at the Louvre and the Bastille.

The pictures of the Eiffel Tower showed a great cage of widely separated steel girders, and it didn't look as though you could blow it up with a bomb. There was nothing much to blow against. So we dropped that one. And pictures I saw of the Louvre showed it filled with statues of women with no arms, and angels with broken wings, and others with no heads, and then just a lot of paintings, so there didn't seem much point in blowing up the Louvre.

But the Bastille was something else, with all the clandestine government activity we knew must be going on there, so secret that you were not even allowed to photograph the building.

So we decided my target would be the Bastille.

And some of you are laughing already because you know, as I know now, that the Bastille had been torn down in 1789 and that is why you can't find any present-day photographs of it. But of course we didn't know that.

It took me six days to get to Paris, by buses and boats and various trains. When I got there with my bomb in my briefcase I was a little confused at first when I came out of the railroad station right into the excitement and bustle of the Big City. I checked in to a little two-star hotel nearby to calm myself down and gather my thoughts together, and after a somewhat restless sleep filled with strange dreams I set out the next day to find the Bastille, with my briefcase in tow.

I saw buses going every which way, and signs on the sidewalk pointing to stairways going down underground to the "Metropolitain." I didn't much like the looks of that but I had my map and thought it was safer to walk, so I set off on foot. I had used maps before, in the hills in Algeria. It took a while but I finally got to what was called the "Place de la Bastille," just like it said on the map. Not a very fancy neighborhood, but otherwise not much different from the other streets and areas I had walked through. The Place de la Bastille had its share of traffic, stores, trees, noise, and in the center a big open plaza area where people were milling around selling fish and vegetables and postcards, and pencils, and blue and white and red flags, as well as shirts and caps and sandals and other things that you can buy just as easily in the markets at Oran not to mention many other places in Paris.

I had to ask someone, "Excuse me, Sir, is it that it is possible that you could perhaps tell me where it is that the Bastille finds itself?"

"This is it, Buddy."

"I mean the building."

"The building? Are you nuts?" He couldn't believe I was serious.

"I just asked you a simple question."

"Well, you're a little late; they tore it down in 1789."

"They did?"

"Yes, they did. *Oui, Monsieur. Détruite. Complètement.*"

"*Alors, merci de toute façon.*" Thanks anyway.

"*Pas de problème.*" No problem.

Well, there was a problem. A dilemma. How to blow up something that did not exist? I couldn't just walk away; I had made a vow and had sworn to carry out my mission. And my reputation as a real man was at stake. I sat down on a bench and tried to think. Then, eureka! It came to me. Maybe I am smarter than I look, because it suddenly became clear what I must do.

What I did was detach the percussion cap from the plastique explosive. I went back to the Seine river and quietly dropped the main body of explosive without the detonator into the water. Then I went back up to the Bastille Plaza, opened the percussion cap, told the children playing there and hanging around looking at me to back off and open up a giant circle, standing well back. Then I set off the percussion cap detonator with a big bang, amid many cheers and hand clapping.

I went back to the little hotel where I was staying and got the concierge to send a telegram from me back to my cronies in Algeria. Of course, I could only tell the truth.

My message read: I HAVE CARRIED OUT INSTRUCTIONS STOP MISSION ACCOMPLISHED STOP MADE A BIG BANG STOP BASTILLE DESTROYED STOP.

As I said, nothing but the truth.

THE END

Epilogue

Because I feared that my friends in Algeria might hold me lower in their estimation when they learned or figured out some day that it was not really I who destroyed the Bastille, I began to think that it might be nice to live here in Paris. By then I had been here less than forty-eight hours but was already beginning to like the place even though it was ten times as big as Oran. So I decided to stay and look for a job and soon found a position as a wine steward in a middle-class restaurant. The name of the owner was Pierre, and - would you believe - he had a daughter named Marie. Same name, different woman. What more could anyone ask for?

I have also visited Les Invalides and seen Napoleon's tomb, been to the Louvre and Notre Dame, and have often enjoyed the view of the Seine from the Pont Neuf, and I even went to the opera once, but I never did figure out why the stupid French have a Place de la Bastille when there is no Bastille. Anyway, I am happy with my life in Paris. I now have both French and Algerian friends here, and another Marie, and on top of that I don't have to worry about proving a point anymore.

Locks of Gold

I had always wanted to go to France, and I finally got the chance when I was twenty-two, my first year out of college. Mom, my step-mother that is, who had cared for me since I was eleven, had been married briefly, when she was very young, to a rich Frenchman, a bigwig in the Peugeot Automobile Company and well known in French society, who left her with quite a bit of money when he died, much of it tied up in France. My father agreed with her view that some post-graduate studies in France would be good for the rounding out of my education, but one condition they both insisted upon was that I must follow a rigid and responsible routine with some serious studies; it was not to be a year of just playing around in Paris. Mom, who still had some connections over there, even went so far as to arrange for sub-let of suitable quarters for me in an elegant apartment house in an old and very proper area on the Left Bank, comprising several rooms complete with all necessary furnishings (and even some unnecessary), including full kitchen loaded with all the appliances, pantry, bathroom, hot water, the works - plus a twenty-four-hour concierge to ensure the maintenance of order and decorum.

My step-mother still subscribed to *Paris Match*, and was not amused to find that, even before I left the shores of the USA for my year abroad, my impending arrival in Paris had gotten a brief mention in the social column of that popular scandal sheet. "Millionaire's son from

America to study at the University of Paris, blah, blah, etc."

Anyway, I was going there to study, so they got that part right, but also to prove that I could get along on my own in a new environment. I admit that I had been rather coddled and, you might even say, spoiled growing up; I certainly had never lacked for anything important or material. So Paris was a challenge that I was looking forward to, to handle by myself - on my own.

The apartment Mom had lined up was quite nice, certainly a lot fancier than I needed, with high ceilings and a view of the garden, in a good location on the rue Chomel off Raspail, not too far from the Boule Miche and the Sorbonne, which is really the University of Paris. The owners did not usually rent to students, but through her contacts Mom had managed to get an exceptional approval for them to accept me. Even after I moved in I never met the owners directly, but nevertheless felt that the concierge was concerned lest a mere student should demean the elegance of the establishment.

But I am quiet and studious by nature, and I was there to learn. I soon set up a regular routine, with classes every day. I devoted three evenings a week to the cafés on the boulevard, but it was to practice my French with students and other people in an informal atmosphere - the real spoken language - and not to booze it up. I rarely drank to excess and always ate moderately. There were plenty of rotisseries and bars and bistros near the school and the area of St. Germain, and I sampled a few, but as I am a creature of habit I soon made my social home at a simple but chatty place called *Chez Pierre,* which I began to visit regularly on Tuesday, Thursday, and Saturday. Sticking to my rigorous schedule, I always came home right at twenty-three thirty, which is half past eleven in real time, slipping in through the gate quietly so as not to wake the neighbors or disturb Mme. Martine, the concierge. I always felt Mme. Martine was constantly watching me like a Mme. LaFarge in a Dickens novel, following my movements whether I saw her or not.

My street was quieter than most in Paris, although only three or four blocks from the big avenues. The walk back to my lodgings was always pleasant, bordered as it was by several little green squares or plots of grass and shrubs and park benches, backed mostly by big dark empty government buildings, banks, insurance offices, places like that, but also some very nice apartment houses with their own inner courtyards and drive-in entrance gates. Not that I had a car, of course; I always walked everywhere. So the street was usually dead after eight p.m. Not all of Paris whoops it up all night long. Actually most people stay up far later in Spain than they do in France.

One Wednesday evening I had been out to supper as usual and had been practicing my French at *Chez Pierre* with some other young guys, talking about anything and everything. In those days not many nice girls went out to bistros and sidewalk cafés and places like that, at least not without a man with them. Sometimes a few girls would come by in a little group, clinging together. Anyway, it was only the beginning of November but there was already a chill in the air that night, with the temperature dipping into the teens, on their scale, which would have been the low forties if, like me, you still think in Fahrenheit. But there was a dampness that my dear step-mother would only have described as "raw." A harbinger of the winter to come.

So on this particular evening I was returning to my lodgings at eleven-thirty as usual, and the street was deserted and getting colder, when I saw what looked like a laundry bag on a sidewalk bench less than a block from where I lived. I stopped for a closer look and was surprised to see the thing move, sit up, and reveal itself to be a young girl of apparently thirteen or fourteen years of age. But what immediately struck me was the torrent of bright golden hair tumbling over her shoulders, reflecting its brilliance even in the dimness of the feeble street light on the corner. Her clothes looked shabby and thin, definitely not a proper outfit for a chilly November evening.

She was the one who broke the silence. "Monsieur," she said, through lips stiff with the cold.

"What are you doing out here? Who are you? Where do you live? How long have you been here?" My questions came fast; I had to do something. No cops in sight, of course. No one, anywhere.

She replied slowly, almost in a stammer, but sort of mysteriously. "I am waiting for tomorrow. I have no place to go. It's a long story." She seemed to have difficulty speaking, in her frail childish voice.

"You must be freezing. Are you hungry?" I didn't know what to say, but felt I had to go on talking. "You can't stay here," I said without thinking, "You'd better come with me."

So I took the skinny waif home with me, trying to slip in quietly through the gate so as not to disturb the neighbors or arouse the omniscient concierge, but at that moment the waif let out a couple of coughs that pierced the silent night like a fog horn, causing the curtains of the concierge window to slide back as though in response to an automatic garage-door opener. For a moment I thought of confronting the concierge myself and turning the waif over to her, but I know what would have happened. She would have put her out into the street and told her to be on her way. But, although it didn't seem important, somehow I was sorry the concierge had seen me and the girl.

So I took her on in, and once home in the apartment, I had a better look at the child - a pretty little thing, hard to tell how old she might have been. But mostly what I saw was her locks of gold, rather unkempt though they were. Although I was tired and sleepy myself, I told her to wash up in the bathroom and warm her hands in the hot water while I heated up some soup and got out some bread and wine for her, as though I were feeding a stray puppy.

She didn't seem to want to talk much, just sat there eating, with a vacant look on her tired face, so I didn't press her. I couldn't bear to put her back out into the street, so I gave her my bedroom and spent the night on the couch. I would hear her story in the morning.

The next day I awoke at the usual time, washed, shaved, and brushed my teeth, then started preparing breakfast, all the time listening for any stirrings from my new guest in the bedroom. Silence. The clock ticked on and soon the time for me to leave for school was approaching. Quietly I opened the bedroom door and peeked in. There she was, sound asleep, with her golden curls spread silently across the pillow - both pillows. "Poor thing," I thought. "I'd better let her sleep on."

But I had to go. So I left a note telling her I had to go to school, but that she could stay there until I got back later that afternoon. I told her to help herself to some breakfast and anything else she wanted.

At school I could not concentrate on my studies, thinking of her and her golden curls and wondering who she was and where she had come from. I was eager to go back and hear her story.

After my last class I hurried home, not even stopping for my customary quaff *Chez Pierre*. It was a 20-minute walk from school.

When I turned into my street, I was most surprised to see two police cars with flashing lights and a small crowd gathering in the middle of the block near my apartment.

"What on earth is going on?" I wondered.

Several policemen on foot were looking over the people in the street and pushing and shoving them around, one by one. I went up to one of the gendarmes and before I could open my mouth he snapped, "And who are you, Monsieur?"

"What is going on?" I asked.

"Look, Buddy, I asked you a question. Who are you?"

"I'm just a student coming back from school. I'm an American citizen," I said protesting, as I instinctively backed away.

"How nice," he said sarcastically, coming right into my face as Frenchmen so often do. "What are you doing here?"

"Doing here?" I muttered. "I live here."

"For the last time, what is your name?"

"My name?" I still didn't get it. "My name is Jimmy Markham."

"Mar - comb? Are you James Markham?"

"Yes. That is correct."

"Monsieur Markham, you are under arrest."

"What for?"

"Kidnapping and suspected rape of a minor."

"What!"

Well, it seems that my know-it-all concierge noted my suspicious behavior coming home with this girl the night before, and reported it to the authorities. At first I thought it was because she didn't want her establishment sullied with any suggestion of its being a place of ill repute. In Paris, can you imagine. Paris, with its free-for-all activities going on all the time, all over the place.

Apparently the police had on hand a report of a missing girl with golden hair, and with great effort were able to put one and one together. I later learned that the morning paper had had an item on a girl with golden hair who had been reported missing two days earlier. Foul play had been suspected. Although I hadn't seen the paper, my concierge must have seen it, and, whether it was fame or fortune she was seeking, she immediately called the police.

Needless to say, I was stunned, almost speechless. Still thinking of that poor young girl, I stammered, "It was her locks of gold . . . I could almost feel them."

"You'll feel some locks, Buddy, locks of steel this time," said the copper, as he slipped on the handcuffs.

They took me to the jail and spent the rest of the evening grilling me with gusto, asking about what had I done with the girl, what other crimes I had committed, and whether I was trying to get ransom money, because, they kindly advised me, "It won't work." I thought of trying to bribe them to let me go, but promptly rejected the idea; it only would have served to prove my guilt. But of course none of my innocent answers gave them any satisfaction, so they locked me up until a court date for a hearing could be scheduled.

So there I was. What to do? I honestly felt that the police would soon realize their mistake and that the girl would turn up somewhere in a day or two, and I would be released. I didn't know who I would call or what good it would do even if they let me have a telephone. I certainly didn't want to bother my parents with this aberration from my normal routine. I was annoyed and mad at the fickle fate that had gotten me into this mess, but not really worried. I had done nothing wrong. Stupid maybe, but nothing wrong. Even the French police must soon realize their error and let me go.

But by the third day I was still wondering and beginning to have serious concerns.

I didn't know much about the French criminal justice system. Are they supposed to guarantee the right to speedy trial and a jury of one's peers? We say we guarantee these things in the United States, but the truth is that we don't always comply with our own words. Who would my peers be in France? Maybe they have Medieval European torture methods to force confessions, like the rack and thumb-screw and water-boarding. Will they make me crawl naked in front of snapping jaws of vicious dogs like Genghis Khan did with his prisoners in the thirteenth century?

The worst of it all was just the not-knowing. But what I did know was that the French took ages to do anything. Their bureaucracy is slower than mañana in Mexico. In France it can take you half an hour to buy a stamp at the post office. The only things they get to on time are their bicycle races and their precious five-to-seven rendezvouses.

I could not get anything out of the silent guards, stoic, stupid, and stultified as they were. When they brought me some slop called food twice a day, they only said, "Here," as though they were talking to their dog. That went on for five days. I should have insisted on talking to a U.S. consular officer, but in my youthful ignorance I didn't even know such people existed.

I tried repeatedly to ask one of the stupid guards what was going on, but they had no interest in talking to me. Zero. Silent as clams. They made their rounds every four hours and made notes in a little notebook they carried. "How long?" I kept asking. Only one of the guards ever said anything. He was on the morning shift and could only give me the not-so-reassuring news that it might be two or three months before my case came to trial. I wish I had studied a little more about *liberté, fraternité,* and *égalité* and the French system of criminal justice. Three months? I couldn't possibly believe that was true.

I did ask if I could make a phone call, even though I still wasn't sure who I wanted to talk to. School, maybe. "You don't need a phone, Buddy. You need to shut up."

About three p.m. on the sixth day, the afternoon guard came by and said I had a visitor. A visitor? Yes, a visitor. Behind him was a little old woman dressed in black with a thick shawl pulled over her head and shoulders and tied under her chin. The guard gave her a stool by the bars of my cell and went on off, leaving her there. I didn't know what to say.

She was the one who broke the silence. "Monsieur," she said. Her voice was strangely familiar, not quite the voice you would expect from a bent old woman.

"Yes? Who are you? What's going on?"

"Monsieur, I think I can help you."

"Help me? What do you mean?"

"I mean, help you get out of here. You do want to get out of here don't you?"

I thought, as they say in Texas when something is obvious, does a cow have an ass? Of course I wanted to get out. So I said, "Of course I want to get out. But who are you? I don't get it."

"I think I can get you out . . . "

"That would be 'super'," I said. (*Super* in French means *splendid, great*.) " . . . But how? I still don't understand."

"A word or two in the right place. But it will cost you something, of course."

"Anything," I said. "Anything to get me out of here."

"It will cost a lot."

"All right. So what. How much is 'a lot,' and how can you do it? Are you a witch or something?" She could have been a Gypsy sorceress, for all I knew. The only thing I *did* know was that I *didn't* know how things were done in France.

The woman spoke clearly and authoritatively, although her voice sounded rather theatrical, as though it had been rehearsed for the stage or for the present occasion.

"It will cost 20,000 Euros. We know all about your step-mother and all her money. You will write to her and tell her to deposit 20,000 Euros in a Swiss bank for which I shall now give you the private account number. And I have the letter-paper here for you to write on. I will mail it for you. You will be out of here one day after the money is deposited. It will only take a word from me to the authorities."

"You are crazy," I said. "Who are you anyway? And what makes you think you can do it?"

And with that she got off the stool and straightened up to her full height of one meter fifty-five centimeters, or five feet one, almost, and drew back her shawl letting a torrent of golden hair cascade over her shoulders.

Yes, it was my little waif who, it seems, was also an actress. Age? Indeterminate, probably somewhere between sixteen and sixty. She certainly wasn't the thirteen-year-old I thought I had been befriending. She could have passed for anything between ten and a hundred and ten, wrapped up in her opaque shawl and bent over like that.

"My God! It's you! You were supposed to have disappeared, and you have been reported missing all this time!" Then I stopped a minute, before going on.

"What is this anyway, some sort of scam?"

"You got that right, Monsieur. *Oui, c'est ça. Précisement.* Eet eez skaaam. Now, zee letter to your step-mother, eef you want to get out of here . . . Now, before zee guard comes back, or eet eez all off."

Somebody in France had found out that my family had some money, how, I don't know; the damned newspaper, I'll bet. I never did like French newspapers; zee International Edition of zee *Herald Tribune* never would have done zat to me.

THE END

Hypocrisy, Anyone ?

I was born in a little town in central Alabama, and I am what most people nowadays would call a racist. Maybe most people are somewhat racist themselves if they are honest about it. Racists or hypocrites. But at least I'll admit it. I don't know whether I was born a racist, or even if that's possible, but I do know I grew up racist. Racist mostly because of my mother. My father died when I was very young, and my mother married the first good thing she could get a hold of, who happened to be a successful young engineer from New Hampshire who had been in Alabama working on a big TVA dam project since the late thirties.

Almost everybody knows something about the Civil War and Reconstruction. At least in Alabama everybody seems to, except that here we call it the War between the States, or, perhaps more aptly, the War for Southern Independence, or, even best of all, the War of Northern Aggression. So my mother was in something of a delicate position, coming from a heritage of impoverished gentility with deep roots in the ante-bellum aristocracy of the Old South, but clinging to a new savior in the form of a New England Yankee who was financially able to make some of her fantasies and dreams of an elegant lifestyle come true once again. Her family, my ancestors, had never recovered from the devastation of the War and the loss of their lands and their plantations, which had been seized to pay for exorbitant and unjust taxes imposed by the Yankees, or sold to cover the cost of Alabama's war debts and expenditures for artificial limbs and the care of disabled Confederate veterans, not to mention the cost of restoring the University at Tuscaloosa, which the Yankees had destroyed along with our libraries and other public buildings and facilities all across the state. After the War, many of the Southern gentlemen who were still left apparently preferred to nurse their pride and go hungry rather than learn a trade; at least that's the way it seems to have been in my family. I believe my mother and my grandparents would rather have been poor than get their hands dirty, although both thoughts were absolutely repugnant to them. They hated anything "unrefined," as my mother would say, especially things like poverty and dirty fingernails.

The way my mother handled her quandary is something that has bothered me most of my life. Always conscious that my step-father was from a Republican state in the heart of the Deep North, she clothed herself in the image of an ardent admirer and lover of Abraham Lincoln. Of course when I was a little older I learned how Lincoln almost singlehandedly brought on the War and took our slaves away from us. Then with my penetrating insight I could see that Mom's pose was clearly just a ploy to curry favor and maintain a good relationship with my step-father. I loved my mother, who was very good to me, caring and nurturing all my life, so it bothered me to see that she was such a hypocrite. I liked my step-father too, but I felt that Mom was betraying the racist heritage that was locked so deep in her nature, and which was always so evident to me in the way she handled the blacks and naturally looked down on them, being, as they were, just one step removed from their origins as uncivilized, savage savages from Darkest Africa. She would condescendingly refer to them as darkies, or colored people, boys, mulattoes, coons, Sambos, spades, tar babies, chocolate drops, Negroes, nigras, and of course niggers and jigaboos, or simply jigs. It wasn't that she disliked them. In fact, she was very fond of some of them, almost like favorite pets. But it was not just my mother that was like this. All of us naturally looked down on the blacks, for we realized that they were on a different level from white people, and we thought it rather amusing when, on occasion, we heard a black man who was angry for some reason lash out and call another black man a "low-down dirty nigger."

It was my mother who first explained to me how it had been necessary for the whites in the South after the War to take certain steps and actions to protect themselves from the threat of ambitious blacks influencing their society and their lives, or trying to get too friendly with their daughters. "Uppity" was the word she used. That is why the Ku Klux Klan and other quiet organizations had to be formed, she told us, to keep the blacks in their place after the new amendments and laws were passed allowing them so much freedom. My mother even had a brother and a brother-in-law who were members of the KKK, and they were pretty high up in the local chapter. The thing I didn't like about the KKK was the stories you occasionally heard of lynchings and hangings of Negroes that had overstepped reasonable bounds. Now I too realized that it was necessary for the Negroes to be kept in line, but I have never supported the death penalty; never felt it was justified for any crime, even wrongdoings committed by black people.

Through my uncles I knew several members of the Klan, and a few years after my mother died I was delighted to hear that a splinter group had been formed, that called itself the Will of God Klan, or WGK. It espoused a program or platform of nonviolent control of racial matters and the keeping of blacks in their place by peaceful means. We weren't very active, but we did make sure the buses and schools and public restrooms in our county stayed nice, and at election time we put up signs around the voting places saying, "If you don't know anything about politics, you shouldn't vote." That sort of thing.

Of course the blacks understood that this was intended for them; anyway the ones that could read did, but the others got the message too, somehow. We made sure that wages for field hands as well as day workers and gardeners and domestics and people like that were standardized for fairness and for the good of the economy. We also kept our local schools and restaurants nice, and were proud of our local churches of whatever type, for they all fully supported our views and activities. We even brought in some of the more intelligent blacks from the community occasionally to attend a special meeting of the Will of God Klan. It was to explain to them the importance of peacefully following God's will as laid down by the Scriptures and the teachings of the principal founding father of the Free Black Movement, whose speeches, paradoxically, gave us guidance in our mission.

This sort of bi-polar society seemed to be stable as long as everybody in our town recognized that there were unwritten laws and customs that it was best to follow. People of all stripes seemed comfortable and happy with life in our community, and that went on quite peacefully for a number of years.

However, after the tumultuous days of President Lyndon Johnson's administration, with new laws that the federal government began imposing on God-fearing communities all over the country, we ran into some trouble. A new federal circuit court judge was appointed for our district, who did not understand Southern society very well. Probably seeking a bit of fame as well as following the dictates of his own misguided conscience and training from the University of Ohio Law School, he zeroed in on the Will of God Klan, which he asserted was unconstitutional or in violation of certain statutes or something. He managed to have the WGK dragged into court on charges of supporting, fomenting, and encouraging racial discrimination and unrest - words like that. And he ordered that the catechism of the Will of God Klan be read in court and that the author of our catechism be identified.

As a representative of the KGB . . . I mean the WGK . . . I was given the dubious honor of obeying this order. So, reluctantly, I started in:

"Your Honor, at the request of the court, I shall now read the catechism, or doctrine, of the Will of God Klan, a private social and cultural organization comprising a limited number of God-fearing individuals dedicated to the development of friendship and the peaceful maintenance of traditional values, a stable society, and a sound economic structure, for the benefit of our entire community:

"ONE: I *am not, nor ever have been, in favor of bringing about in any way the social and political equity of the white and black races.*

"TWO: *I am not nor ever have been in favor of making voters or jurors of Negroes, nor of qualifying them to hold office, nor to intermarry with white people.*

"THREE: *There is a physical difference between the white and black races which I believe will forever forbid the two races living together on terms of social and political equality.*

"FOUR: *There must be the position of the superior and the inferior; and I, as much as any other man, am in favor of the superior position being assigned to the white man.*"

You could have heard a pin drop.

The judge grunted, frowned, and then roared out: "And who was the author of these abominations you have had the effrontery to present here today? He should be executed! And shot! I would like to have him brought before this court!"

"I am sorry, your Honor, we cannot do that. The author has already been shot, and is already dead. He died in 1865. His name was Lincoln. Abraham Lincoln. He said all these things in 1859, the year before he was elected President of the United States of America and four years before his famous speech calling for Malice toward None, and Charity for All."

THE END

Epilogue

The judge had little choice but to dismiss the case. The Will of God Klan was left intact for the moment, but since then, over the years, it has faded considerably in size and importance, and is now all but extinct.

Sometimes I wonder whether my mother, who joined Lincoln in the Heavenly Kingdom many years ago, even before the Will of God Klan was founded, might possibly have known more about Lincoln than she let on - more than any of us ever knew at the time. Or whether she was, as I still believe, just another hypocrite.

You Took the Words

As I have said before, I am a pretty ordinary guy, I think. Oh, I know everybody is different in their way, but there is certainly a range of normalcy. What we call normal.

Anyway, this could have happened to anybody, but maybe not just the way it happened to me.

I was born and raised in the suburbs of Toledo, Ohio where I had an active life like all the kids in our neighborhood. I loved sports and started playing football in Jones High School, and then went to college at Ohio State University in Columbus, where of course I also tried out for the team. But as you may know, football is big at OSU, very big. There it was a different ballgame, so to speak; the players were all giants and were practically pros already. I had some fun in practice knocking about with them, working out, scrimmaging, and running the plays, but I was always second string. In four years I only got into one 'varsity' game, and that was because we were beating Akron 55 to 2 in the fourth quarter and the coach must have figured that even my feebleness was not so great as to risk losing the game for us at that point. What I loved about football was not just the game itself but the image it gave you with the girls. The girls around the campus loved all the football players and let them know it. If you were a football player you could spill ketchup on your shirt or mumble in your beer and still make out. And I as much as anyone enjoyed maintaining that image.

I majored in accounting, but the girls I knew - or young women as they prefer to be called nowadays - were always more impressed by football players than by accountants. And for many years I always wore my football pin in my lapel so the women would know me for the he-man I really was, or at least wanted to be.

After graduation I got a job with an accounting firm back in Toledo, where I could be near my parents, and soon thereafter I married the girl who had lived next door, in the house right next to ours. Sally Richards was her name.

We've been married almost ten years now, and have two daughters, nine and five. Sally is a beautiful woman - she was our high school homecoming queen her senior year - but nevertheless I am proud to say she has been a faithful wife and a good housekeeper and a good mother to our children. Like many beautiful women, she never had to stretch her brain much to make it successfully through school and through life. As "popular" as she was in high school, I think the main reason she chose me was because I played football but weighed only 185 pounds and didn't have a broken nose. She was a little 104-pounder, and the big guys who weighed 250 or 275 would have mashed her flat.

There was never anything really wrong with our marriage, and probably the worst thing I could say about it is that at times it was a little boring. I don't know how else to explain all that happened.

Although I am well established with the accounting firm in Toledo, part of my responsibilities include supervision of certain operations we have going on in Cleveland, which require my spending one week in

Cleveland each month. At first I just stayed at a hotel, but then found it much more comfortable and convenient and no more expensive to rent a furnished apartment downtown. And, would you believe, I met another woman in Cleveland after I had been there only two or three times. Her name was Betty something. She was really gorgeous; she told me she had been runner-up in the Ohio Miss America contest a few years ago, and I could see why. Now she too was married, but she never told me anything about her husband except that he also was an accountant. Small world. But I didn't know him; Cleveland is a big city. Interesting how small the world is and how big the cities are.

Well, you know, for an active young man, especially a football player, to go for a whole week without a woman would be asking an awful lot, and, as this young woman seemed to like me, I started seeing her, and pretty soon we were making out on a regular basis, one week per month, when I was in Cleveland. It was no big deal; I still loved my wife just the same as always, but Betty filled a gap in my life, and I seemed to fill a gap in hers, so to speak. I think you could say that we liked each other and were even fond of each other but certainly weren't in love or anything like that. We just enjoyed each other's company and enriched each other's life for a few days each month. That's about the way it was, and that went on for nearly two years.

Then just last month something happened that you will not believe. There was a big convention of accountants in Columbus that lasted for three days. Speeches, lectures, presentations of new high-tech accounting and auditing techniques, and of course lots of office machines and computer programs and spread sheets. Then there was a big final cocktail party in the ballroom Sunday night, with a tremendous crowd of people, where I must confess I got a little tight. I had brought my wife with me, and she was getting along fine, gabbing away with several other ladies when I went to refill my drink at the bar. It was then that I spotted Betty in the same room, off to one side. I had no idea that she and her husband were coming to Columbus; she had never mentioned this convention and I guess I hadn't either. Anyway, there she was, some distance away, looking radiant as usual, not far from where my wife was standing. "Oh well," I thought, in my relaxed state, "So what?"

There was no reason for it to surprise me. The Ohio Accountants and Auditors Association OAAA - "Ooo-Waa" we used to call it - covered the entire state, and had brought people in from all over, three or four hundred, plus optional wives, for this gathering. But as you can understand, I didn't need to confront Betty right there in front of my wife, and I am sure Betty would have felt the same way. Actually, as I saw them there, I felt quite a sense of pride welling up within me, enjoying the thought that I had possessed the two most beautiful women in the room.

So I was feeling pretty good about myself right then as I was getting my refill at the bar. And, being a little tight, and in an expansive mood, I couldn't help saying something to the fellow next to me, also getting himself anther drink:

"Nice party, what?" I led off.

"Yep. Nice party."

"Some lovely women here," I continued.

"Yep, sure are."

"Say, you see those two women over there in the corner?"

"Where?"

"Over there. One in the long black dress and the other in red."

He turned his head. "Yeah, sure. What about them?"

"Well, not bad, eh?"

"No, not bad. In fact, they are both pretty good looking."

"Gorgeous, I would say."

"All right. Gorgeous."

I moved a little closer: "Well, I'll tell you something."

"Yeah, what?"

"Well," I said with my voice lowered but puffed up with modest pride, "one of them is my mistress and the other is my wife."

He smiled and looked at me, not with the awe and admiration I expected, but with an expression of tolerance and condescension: "You took the words right out of my mouth."

THE END